Reaching up, she placed her hand against his cheek.

"Thank you, Leo."

He caught her fingers and planted a soft kiss into her palm. "No, thank you. Since Susan died, holidays of any sort have been difficult for me. Maybe if we had been blessed to have had those two children who were almost ours. . ." He sighed.

Feelings of inadequacy flooded back in, wiping out all the contentment that the ride home had lent to Martha. She had watched him with Melissa and Luke's children. If any man should be a father, it was this one. He shouldn't be wasting his time with her, a woman past childbearing years. He should be dating a younger woman, one who could give him the children he so obviously desired. Wasn't procreation one of the main reasons for marriage, after all?

Even though she was breaking on the inside and her throat felt like dry toast, she had to agree. "Having those two little loves would have made a big difference, Leo." She licked her lips, unsure as to whether she should go on, the topic being deeply personal. But she knew that she had to. Before they took their relationship any further, this was something they had to discuss. "You're a man and. . .you can still. . .have children. If"—her voice dropped to a whisper—"you have the right woman."

MELANIE PANAGIOTOPOULOS, born in Richmond, Virginia, currently resides in Athens, Greece, with her husband of nearly twenty-five years. They have two children. Melanie has done extensive research into the early-Christian and medieval period of history and has published numerous articles on both subjects, something which is reflected in her books. To be where the early Christians and especially that great apostle to the Gentiles, Paul, worked and lived has inspired her greatly. She has spent many weekends with her family exploring little-known sites and many a winter morning sifting through dusty, but fantastic, books at some of the wonderful, old libraries Athens has to offer.

Books by Melanie Panagiotopoulos

HEARTSONG PRESENTS

HP217—Odyssey of Love
HP261—Race of Love
HP321—Fortress of Love
HP505—Happily Ever After
HP558—A Fairy-Tale Romance

In a Land Far, Far Away

Melanie Panagiotopoulos

Heartsong Presents

To my dear friends Zaira Andoniadis, Helen Salter, and
Valery Zandona: My three stalwart encouragers. Thank
you, dear friends, for all your help and encouragement
throughout the years. Much love to you all.

A note from the author:
I love to hear from my readers! You may correspond with me
by writing:

> **Melanie Panagiotopoulos**
> **Author Relations**
> **PO Box 719**
> **Uhrichsville, OH 44683**

ISBN 1-59310-064-7

IN A LAND FAR, FAR AWAY

Our mission is to publish and distribute inspirational products offering
exceptional value and biblical encouragement to the masses.

All of the characters and events in this book are fictitious. Any resem-
blance to actual persons, living or dead, or to actual events is purely
coincidental.

one

Martha clapped her hands together. "Now it's my turn to have news for all of you," she said to her family and friends, who were gathered in the kitchen of what had been her home for all of her fifty-six years. But her news was soon to change that.

"News?" Natalia, Martha's much younger sister, asked with a tilt of her famous blond head. "What news?" she persisted, and Martha took the moment to regard her sister.

She knew that the fondness she felt for Natalia had to be evident in her face. Natalia was Martha's adoptive sister, but because Martha was thirty-two years her senior, Martha thought of her more as a daughter than as a sister. And just as a mother might feel upon the return of her child for a holiday, Martha had loved having Natalia and her husband, Noel, home for these few days.

The Pappas family had adopted Natalia when she had only been a few weeks old. Although their mamma had been beyond her childbearing years and their father—*Baba*—had been quite old to be the father of an infant, Martha doubted that any girl could have been showered with more love than Natalia while being raised in the village of Kastro in Greece.

"*Ella, koukla mou*—come, my doll. What is it?" *Baba* encouraged when Martha didn't immediately speak. Martha turned to her father. Her smile deepened. Although the calendar declared him to eighty-five years old, he was as thin and spry as a man half his age might be. Only the gray of his beard, the deep crinkles around his eyes, and the rasp of his voice indicated his advanced age.

As did his wisdom.

He was the wisest man Martha knew, and when people compared her to him—as they often did—they extended to her the ultimate compliment. But right now she liked the way her *Baba* still referred to her as *"koukla mou."* How many fifty-six-year-old women had fathers who called them "my doll"?

Hurriedly rising from her seat next to the recently white-washed and now flower-bedecked *tzaki*—fireplace—she went over to the sink and to the curtains that fluttered in the soft May breeze above it. She tied back the light floral fabric.

"What news, Martha?" Allie, the village physician, asked from her place beside her husband, but when Martha only turned back to her friends and family and smiled, Allie flicked her long French braid behind her shoulder and gave a slight laugh before continuing. "Honestly, Martha. I've never known you to take so long to say or do something."

That brought chuckles of concurrence from all, and Martha couldn't keep one from escaping her own lips either. She knew that Allie hadn't meant it in any way unkindly.

Besides, Martha knew that she was taking a long time. Especially for her. She was normally as quick as a buzzing bee in both speech and action.

"Well, this decision took quite awhile to arrive at, so it deserves to be stated slowly." She took a deep breath and swallowed down the unfamiliar butterflies that were flittering around in her stomach. But somehow the proverbial butterflies were pleasant too, because they meant that there was soon to be an exciting and new adventure in her life. And that thrilled Martha as much as if she were a child going off to school for the first time. "And even more I want you all to know that I have said many prayers concerning it, and I'm certain that I'm moving in God's will for my life by following through on it."

"Martha. . ." Natalia groaned and clasped her long, slender hands together. "I promise that I won't ever tease you about being too quick again. Tell us!"

But Martha still didn't, immediately. She took her time and regarded the two couples. Except for her father, who was a longtime widower, she was the only single person in the group. But that was not something that had ever bothered her. Her unmarried state had never given her cause for alarm because she had lived a very fulfilling and free life without the "bonds" of matrimony. First, she had been the youngest of five siblings, then, when all of her older brothers and sisters had married and moved to various towns and cities, Natalia had joined the family. Because of Mamma's long illness and subsequent death, the primary care of both the baby girl and her Mamma had fallen upon her, something Martha had never minded.

Natalia was now a world-renowned fashion model living in New York with her husband, Noel. Her father had found joy in spending his time between Natalia in America, her brothers and sisters in Athens, and her in Kastro. But Martha knew that because of the research he was doing for a book about the early teachers of the church—a dream of his forever—that he only spent time in Kastro because she was there. And that was silly, especially since Martha had been led to follow a dream of her own.

"I'm going to be opening a shop in Ancient Olympia," she

blurted out and had the satisfaction of seeing every mouth in the kitchen drop open in shock.

She laughed.

Then happy pandemonium broke out as everyone started laughing and talking and congratulating her all at once.

Natalia squealed and pulled her into a hug. "So that's the reason you've been going to Olympia nearly every week to visit our relatives there."

Martha squeezed her tall and slender sister back tightly. Even with Natalia living an ocean and a continent away, they were so intuitively connected. She should have known that Natalia would figure that out quickly. "Exactly. And I have grown to love the town. It's where our mamma's ancestors hail from, after all." Martha knew that along with its history, and the peaceful, thoughtful quality of the green and fertile valley in which the ancient site was situated, that was one of the things that made Olympia so appealing to her. Her mother had grown up there. She had only left the town of Ancient Olympia when she had married.

"How absolutely wonderful! And exciting," Allie exclaimed. "So similar to my own adventure when I first came to Kastro."

Martha grimaced, remembering back to Allie's reception to the village. "Well, I hope the people of Olympia are a bit more friendly to me than Kastro's population was to you!"

Stavros groaned, and his dark eyes narrowed in guilt. "Don't remind me." The village schoolteacher, he had been one of those who had tried to get Allie to leave those first days after her arrival.

His wife nudged him and, slanting her eyes at him, said, "But you soon came to your senses, Darling."

His mouth twisted downward in remorse for his behavior

before he leaned toward her and gave her a quick kiss. "That I did," he agreed. Then to Martha he said, "With you moving to Ancient Olympia, at least I know where to bring the kids for a field trip next year."

"You better." That idea pleased Martha. It would be a connection with her home that she would treasure.

The only thing Martha had left to do to make her move official was to sign the papers for the property on Ancient Olympia's main street. She had fallen in love with the meticulously restored traditional Greek town house. The ground floor was meant to be a shop, while a two-bedroom apartment with polished plank floors, recessed, shuttered windows, as well as vine-covered verandas for living was above it. Compared to most of the town's buildings, which were post–World War II, nondescript, flat-roofed structures of concrete and glass, it was a real find.

But without her father's blessing, she wouldn't follow through with her plans. Martha turned. *"Baba?"*

His lips moved a moment in the sweet way of older men filled with emotion before words came out. "I am so proud of you, *kali mou kori*—my dear daughter," he rasped. "You were a wonderful girl, and you have grown into one of the most thoughtful and elegant of women. You have done nothing but bring joy into all of our lives every single day with your sunny smile and your quick and sure ways."

Behind the lenses of his glasses tears touched upon his fine old lashes. But Martha wasn't concerned. She knew her *baba* well enough to know that this moisture came from joy, not sorrow.

"I feel that God has many more wonderful things in store for you, *kali mou.*" He reached out for her hand with his right one and, looking over at Natalia, motioned for his youngest child to take his other. Leaving her place beside Noel, Natalia quickly did so. Squeezing his two youngest children's hands close against his heart, he spoke to Martha. "I am only thankful that you have the faith to make this change in your life. Since I spend so much time in Athens and New York, leaving you behind in Kastro has weighed heavily on my mind."

"But your following your dream of writing a book and having to spend time away from here to research it is the reason I feel free to pursue my own dream, *Baba*. Moving to Ancient Olympia and opening a shop there is something I have wanted to do for a very long time."

She turned to Natalia, who had been extremely generous with the money she'd earned from high fashion modeling. "I've saved practically all the money that you've given to me though the years." She glanced down at her linen suit and grimaced. "With the exception of having spent quite a nice amount on clothes."

Chuckles were shared around the room, and Martha knew that it was because she had become touted, quite unexpectedly, as one of the most stylish and fashionably in-tune women in Kastro, and the surrounding area as well.

It had all started when, having more than enough of her own, Natalia had asked designers in New York to send clothing to her sister in Kastro. After several box loads of designer clothes arrived in Kastro, Martha soon discovered that she liked the way fine fabric felt against her skin and how well-designed clothes fit her figure. The garments made her feel womanly and feminine in ways she liked. It was one of the few frivolous things she had allowed into her life and one for which she felt no compunction.

"So." She flashed them all a bright smile, refusing to feel

self-conscious. "Other than buying clothes, I have saved everything. I have more than enough to buy and open my own gift shop and keep it running for the next two years, even should I not make a profit." Her gaze returned to her father's. "Your travels between your children's homes and your work is the catalyst directing me on this adventure. For the first time ever, I feel free to pursue something different. Not that I have been unhappy in the life I have led until now, *Baba*. I haven't," she qualified quickly. She had no regrets about the years spent caring for her father's home. She had always thought it a privilege.

"Don't worry, Martha. I understand what you're saying. The truth is"—he looked at her above his glasses—"you are free now. And I am proud of you for following the path God has laid out for you. Natalia did that, and look where it led her."

"Straight to Noel's arms!" Allie sang out, and with a great big smile of concurrence, Natalia left her father's side and went back to Noel's arms.

Noel smiled as he held his wife tightly against his side. "Unfortunately, it took a few years, plus"—he glanced down at the German shepherd that reclined by their feet—"having Prince here as a chaperon." They all knew the story. Natalia and Noel had seen each other for several consecutive years at the same place—Rockefeller Center in New York City at Christmastime—before they even got up the nerve to talk to each other. And that was using Prince as the excuse.

But this line of thought concerned Martha, and a frown pulled her brows together as she returned to her chair. She leaned over and picked up her Siamese cat, Needlepoint. The cat had done her favorite trick of jumping up on Martha's seat as soon as Martha had vacated it. They had all been amazed at how the cat and the dog could be in the same house together, even more, in the same room. But the two animals had been tolerant of one another from the first, even friendly.

Martha placed her cat on her lap and rubbed her feline friend's silky fur while Needlepoint went in a circle to settle herself. "I don't want you all to think that I'm moving to Olympia in order to search for a—" Martha had to swallow, and even then she stumbled over the final word of the sentence, "hus. . .band."

"Why not?" Allie, always the hopeful realist, asked, with a twinkle in her soft eyes. "Do you feel as if you are too old for romance?"

"And if you do, then that's just silly," Natalia interjected.

"No, of course not. Age has nothing to do with it." Martha defended her position. "But Jesus' response to his disciples' question about marriage as recorded in the nineteenth chapter of the Gospel of Matthew does. I think it fits perfectly for my life. Among other things He said, '"others have renounced marriage because of the kingdom of heaven. The one who can accept this should accept it."'"

"Bah," her father softly intoned, and Martha turned back to him in surprise. "I disagree, Martha-Mary." She didn't expect that response from him. And the use of her two names was a sure indication as to how serious he was, even if his voice remained as calm and sweet as always. He only used both her names when he wanted her full attention.

"I don't think that verse refers to you at all." He spoke to her more as *Papouli*—the village priest—than that of father to his child. "To renounce something means that you have given up all rights to it. I don't think you have done that; rather, I think that the man you are to marry has not yet come into your life. You have been needed in this home for so long—God only knows how much we all needed you"— he qualified—"that you are confusing service to your family with that of having renounced marriage."

Shock reverberated through Martha. She had had no idea that her father thought that the man she was to marry hadn't yet—yet—come into her life and that was the reason she hadn't married. Placing Needlepoint on the floor, Martha hurriedly moved to her father's side again and, taking his thin hands in her own, said, *"Baba,* I have never been unhappy in being single. I've led a very fulfilling life, and I'm not moving to Olympia to look for a husband. I'm not unhappy in who I am."

He looked at her above his glasses. "I know that."

"Then?" She was confused.

Between his beard and his mustache his lips curved into a kind smile. "I'm only taking issue with your using that verse in Matthew in respect to your life," he said with that playful twinkle in his intelligent eyes that she so loved in him. "I feel you are misapplying it."

"Oh." She had lived with her father long enough to know better than to discount anything he might say. So clamping down on her ready protest, she listened. His words astounded.

"As Solomon wrote, 'There is a time for everything, and a season for every activity under heaven.' " He reached out and, as he had done a million times before, ran his hand in a father's loving way across her cheek. "If you want to use a verse from the nineteenth chapter of Matthew in reference to your life, Martha-Mary, then I think the correct one might be, 'with God all things are possible.' Even the fulfilling of my longtime prayer for you: that a wonderful man might come into your life so that you, the most deserving of women and the most selfless, might know the joys of married life, just as I was privileged to know with your dear mother—God rest her soul."

Martha was speechless. Literally. A very unusual occurrence for her. She had had no idea that her father had been praying for a partner for her. Her tongue, which normally worked as quickly as her hands, remained still as her father continued.

"None of us would have had the wonderful life we have enjoyed without your ministrations and care. You embody all the good characteristics of Jesus' friends Martha and Mary. Your mother and I named you well when we gave you the double names of Martha-Mary. Even though we call you only by the first part of your name, you are both Martha and Mary. You are Martha, the tireless worker and hostess, and you are Mary, the one who sits at the feet of Jesus and learns from Him. More than anything, moving to Ancient Olympia will give you more time to be a Mary, and for that I am glad."

Martha felt tears—those coming from being profoundly touched and edified by her father—form in her eyes. She knew that her father had always appreciated her running his home since the day her mother had taken ill almost three decades earlier, but she had never realized just how much until this moment. She blinked the moisture away. "*Baba*, I don't know what to say."

He chuckled, a deep, throaty sound, and patted her hand. "Just say that you will take care of you, of Martha, just as you have always taken care of us. And. . .that you will let God lead you in this wonderful new path He is taking you down. . .every step of the way. Even if the steps seem uneven to you at times."

She blinked, and leaning over she put her arms around his skinny, but very strong, shoulders and whispered into his ear, "I will, *Baba*. I promise."

two

Two Months Later

"Hello." Martha's heart seemed to do a double beat at the sound of the voice, the rounded and full, masculine one with which she was becoming familiar. She knew before looking who was standing above her: the man she had often said "Hello" to as they passed one another in and around Ancient Olympia.

As she raised her eyes from the verses in the Bible she had been reading into the deep-set eyes of the tall and slender man, she willed her pulse to slow down. She normally saw him while in motion, either while walking in opposite directions or as he whirled past her on his fancy bicycle. His features were every bit as fine and classical as she had thought, even with lines, made from both smiling often and time, permanently etched into the skin around his mouth. Probably a little bit younger than she, he had the look of a man who had always been in top physical form. His hair was dark and thick with silvery feathers of gray at his temples and behind his ears. It lent him that distinguished look men past the age of fifty who were still in good physical shape were blessed to wear.

And as always, when in his presence, she felt her heart pound against her chest in a very unusual, but exciting, way. She was beginning to think it was anything but abnormal to feel this way around this man. It happened every time she saw him, which had been nearly every day of the two months she had lived in Ancient Olympia. Seeing him had become a highlight of her day.

She returned his smile, but she sincerely hoped that it didn't appear as wobbly as she felt on the inside. "Hello."

He motioned toward the ancient piece of stone masonry that she had made into her bench. "Mind if I join you?"

Martha scanned the tree-filled grounds of the archeological site of Olympia. Brightly clothed tourists, dressed for summer fun in Greece, formed splashes of bold coloring against the pastoral setting as they inspected the jutting columns and low foundations that, with just a little bit of imagination, told of how magnificent the ancient precinct had been once upon a time. Since she was hardly alone, Martha scooted over and offered him the place beside her. "I'd like that."

"I'd like that?" Had she—cautious Martha—actually said that? She was only glad Natalia wasn't around to hear her. How often had she warned her sister when she had first moved away from Kastro against talking to strangers? But Martha wryly remembered that it hadn't done any good. Natalia and Noel had first talked to one another at Rockefeller Center in New York City the previous November: two strangers who ventured to converse. And now look. Not even a year later they had been married for several months.

The man lowered his tall frame to the bench, and turning to face her, he smiled, a smile full of white teeth that matched the gleaming of the columns of the site, with eyes that flashed silver green like the olive trees in the grove. And Martha forgot all about Natalia.

"Since we both seem to live in Ancient Olympia, and we see one another every day—" He had noticed that too! "—I thought that it was time that I stopped and introduced myself. I'm Leo Jones," he said and extended his hand.

Martha looked at it for a moment before placing her much smaller one within it. But when she did, her mouth almost couldn't form her own name. If she thought seeing him and greeting him did things to her, it was nothing as compared to the way his hand enfolding her own made her feel. For the first time ever, she was cognizant of the calluses that a lifetime of cleaning, mending, and activity had added to her hands. At that moment she wished for Natalia's soft, pearly smooth, picture-perfect hands.

She was just noticing that he had even larger calluses on his palms, though, when he prompted, "And you are?"

Martha felt as if all the blood in her body had decided to convene for a convention in her face. She was reacting like a silly schoolgirl. She hadn't even behaved like that when she had been a schoolgirl. But then there had never been a boy in Kastro who had made her feel the way this man did, as if her very being was somehow tied to his. All the boys she had grown up with had felt like brothers or cousins. This man most definitely did not.

"I'm Martha Pappas."

"Martha," he repeated and seemed to taste the individual sonances and nuances belonging to its two syllables. "A name of substance. As well as being pretty, it belonged to one of my favorite Bible characters too."

Her brows shot up to almost meet the brim of her straw sun hat. If she had been wearing sunglasses, they would have risen above the rim. "Martha is one of your favorites? Martha? Mary and Lazarus's sister?" she returned quickly, wanting to make sure that they referred to the same person, even though she didn't think that there was another Martha mentioned in the Bible.

"That's the one."

"Martha normally gets bad press in the story about her in the tenth chapter of Luke." She patted her white, leather-bound Bible. "It's her sister, the contemplative Mary, who most admire."

"I respect her too," he was quick to qualify.

"Then?" She pushed her chin-length hair behind her ears. The stiff breeze was blowing from behind the bench and pushing it into her eyes.

He spoke quickly and with a degree of knowledge that intrigued her. "I don't think of them as being on opposing teams," he began. "We need both Marthas and Marys in the world, but even more, Martha had to learn from Mary, and Mary had to learn from Martha. I think that was the most important lesson taught by that story: one of balancing life."

"Balancing life. . . ," she commented. "That's an interesting thought." And a very good one.

He smiled and continued. "It might seem that by Jesus' saying ' "Martha, Martha. . .you are worried and upset about many things, but only one thing is needed. Mary has chosen what is better. . ." ' that He was reprimanding her for complaining that her sister wasn't helping in the preparation of the food. But I don't think His words were intended just for Martha of Bethany but rather for all the wonderful Marthas—ladies—throughout time who have served their families and made home a wonderful and safe haven of harmony." He squinted out over the site before continuing. "I think the Lord was telling all homemakers who might read about Martha and Mary to calm down and to not be distracted in their walk with Him by the day-to-day activities and stresses that can so easily overwhelm. In other words"—he flashed a quick grin her way—"one pot roast instead of three entrees is better so that they can then have the time to sit at His feet and eat spiritual food. That was something Martha obviously learned, as we can see from her declaration a few months later, as recorded in the twenty-seventh verse of John, chapter eleven, when she answered Jesus, '"I believe that you are the Christ, the Son of God, who was to come into the world."'"

Martha was impressed. This was a man who clearly knew the Bible. And one who was quick to get his thoughts across. She really liked that. "That sounds like something my father might say." She thought. "Hmm. . .has said, even. But he's a very wise, old man." She turned so that she could look directly at the man named Leo Jones. "How did you come to be so smart?" She couldn't believe she had asked that. It was the closest to flirting she had ever come.

"My wife."

Wife. Wife. Wife. The cicadas in the Aleppo pine above them seemed to scream out the refrain as fingers of mortification crawled up Martha's spine. That's what she got for being so bold with a stranger. She should have listened to her own advice to Natalia. She shouldn't have talked to someone in this way with whom she hadn't been properly introduced. What had come over her? She shouldn't have talked to him in this flirtatious way. Period.

But of course this man had to have a wife.

The women of the world would have had to be blind to leave him alone. Even she, of all people, was attracted to him. But she wouldn't, nor couldn't, allow herself to covet another woman's husband. That was something she had never done, and at fifty-six years of age, nearly fifty-seven, it was not something she would start now.

But why, why did she have to be so attracted to him? For

the first time she really understood her young friend Maria and her dilemma with Dimitri Drakopoulos. Maria had been crazy about Dimitri all her life. But Dimitri had only had eyes for Natalia. . .

Martha had never really understood that attraction bug, that thing some called chemistry.

Until this moment.

And she found herself bitten by it. That she was highly attracted to, drawn to, fascinated by this man, by this stranger who was sitting beside her, was not something she could deny.

But he was a married man.

Off limits.

Totally.

She would remove herself from his company before the seed of temptation could be planted even a centimeter deep into the matter of her mind. Gathering her purse and Bible close to her in preparation to leave, she replied, "Your wife sounds like a very smart lady."

"She was."

Martha stopped in the motion of arising and looked closely at his face. Was? Was?

Yes, was.

Definitely past tense.

She could see the truth of it in the reflective, steely color in his deep eyes. It was the same opaque sorrow that she had often seen in her father's over the loss of her mother.

The world seemed to stand still as sadness moved in to replace the guilt of thinking she was attracted to another woman's husband. Martha sat back and hesitated over the question. "Your wife. She has. . .passed on?"

He nodded, took a deep breath, and turning his head to the

right, looked out over what had been the Altis—the sacred precinct of Olympia. But Martha was certain that he wasn't seeing the home of the original Olympic Games as he murmured, "Six years ago."

Her eyes shut briefly. The pain of losing his wife was in the pronunciation of each vowel, each syllable. She recognized it as the same sound that had come from her father and friends in Kastro who had lost their mates.

"I know it's inadequate, but I'm so sorry."

He breathed out deeply and narrowed his eyes. "Thanks." He sat back. "And thanks, too, for not immediately assuming that my referring to my wife in the past tense meant that we were divorced." His head moved up and down softly in a contemplative way. "I know people don't mean to, but it hurts when they immediately assume that my Susan and I could have ever stopped loving one another." He stretched his long legs out in front of him and heaved a heavy sigh. "I know it's just a sign of the times in which we live, with people so lightly sharing wedding vows. But it can really hurt."

"It never even crossed my mind," she murmured. It hadn't.

A sudden smile filled the lines around his mouth. "Where do you come from? Must be somewhere the rest of the world hasn't touched."

She laughed softly. If Kastro was anything, it was that. Not one couple had ever divorced there. "Actually it is. I was born and raised and, until two months ago, lived all my life in a village called Kastro. It's about two hours by car from here." She pointed toward the north. "As a crow flies, just over that broad range of mountains."

He did a double take. "You're not American?"

She tilted her head to the side. The question surprised her.

"Why would you think that?"

"Your English is superb." He gave a little laugh. "Probably better than most native speakers'."

"Thanks." Several Americans, Brits, and Australians who had visited her shop—had told her that. "I like the study of languages. And especially"—she grimaced guiltily—"grammar."

"Ouch." He tapped the heel of his hand against his brow as if he had just been hit. "That's my nightmare."

She had heard that from many people. But it seemed inconceivable to her. "Grammar is like a puzzle to me. I really enjoy it."

"So you've been studying English all your life?"

"No. Actually, on a formal basis, just for the last six years."

He stared at her, and his eyes narrowed as if he had a hard time believing it. "Are you serious? But you speak it so well."

His praise made all the years of hard study worth it in a way nothing else ever had. And that was saying something, since she had had many compliments about her ability to learn foreign languages, and even more, to get the accents down perfectly. Needing to do something with her hands, she let her fingers play with the leather of her purse strap. "When my younger sister moved to America, I started studying English," she explained. "I didn't want her to fall in love someday, marry an American, and find myself unable to communicate with her husband."

"And did she? Fall in love and marry?"

Martha smiled as the image of Natalia and Noel on their wedding day went through her mind. Wearing a wedding gown that she herself had designed, Natalia had not only looked like the famous cover girl she was but like the heroine in the most perfect fairy tale too. She had had a fairy-tale romance with Noel, so Martha hadn't expected anything less. "Noel and Natalia married last March. And now a baby is on the way." They had told her the blessed news just the previous evening during their weekly phone conversation. That new little human was whom she had been praying about—while using the words of the Bible—when Leo had walked up to her.

"A baby. . .how wonderful," he responded, and she thought that she detected a wistful quality, almost one of sadness, before he looked at her in a speculative way, almost with apprehension framing his eyes. A mix of diverse emotions, it confused her. "And how about you?" He asked with an edge to his voice. "Are you married?"

Then she understood.

And she could hardly believe it.

What she now saw in his face was the same anxiety she had felt when she had thought he had a wife. He was afraid that she had a husband! In the same way that the wind touched the leaves on the poplar trees that shaded them, so could she feel his trepidation. It was a heady experience. Slowly she shook her head. "No, Leo," she spoke his given name, feeling that the moment deserved it. "I've never been married."

His eyes softened, and he regarded her as if. . .if. . .she was the most beautiful woman on earth! She couldn't believe that he might actually be as attracted to her as she was to him. "Where have all the men in Kastro been?" His voice was husky, almost a caress.

Excitement, thrilling and grand, coursed through her veins. But pushing right behind it, like one of the floods that had covered the land where they now sat for centuries, came unease. A deep, chilling discomfort that she might be falling for a "line" that was older even than the civilization that had flourished almost three millennia earlier where they now sat assailed her. Goose bumps pricked her skin.

She was acting like an ingénue. She might not be very experienced in the ways of men on a personal level, but she was a mature woman who had seen enough of life to know very well the consequences of trusting unwisely.

In her haste to stand, she dropped her Bible. He reached down and dusted it off on his jeans before standing and giving it back to her. He was looking down at her curiously, undoubtedly trying to understand her sudden change of attitude.

But it wasn't something she was prepared to explain. He was, after all, still a stranger.

"I must go," she said quickly and motioned in the direction of the modern town that was about a half a mile in the distance. "My cousins are expecting me for dinner this evening." She felt safer letting him know that she had family close by. But even as she did, she knew that she was being ridiculous. Deep down she was certain that she didn't ever have to fear this handsome, courteous gentleman. Because he was just that: a gentle man.

He didn't challenge her abrupt change in attitude or manner but instead, with a tilt of his head, indicated the long broad path that led to what was both the entrance and the exit of the ancient site. "May I walk with you? To the exit," he qualified, and she liked the way he didn't ask to see her home. He seemed to understand that she needed time to become acquainted with him.

As she looked up at him and watched the hopeful expression on his face, she knew that to get to know him was something she really wanted too.

Coming on top of her momentary apprehension, it was one of the most incredible feelings she had ever experienced.

three

After a long moment, she nodded. She didn't trust the emotion he might hear in her voice if she spoke.

Seeming to understand her unease and wanting to calm her, he glanced around at their location and motioned to what remained of the early Christian basilica to their left. "It's beautiful here. So peaceful. I find it poignant, too, that Olympia, which was built in honor of mythological gods, should have a Christian basilica upon the very spot where Zeus's seated statue—one of the seven wonders of the ancient world—had been sculpted by the master craftsman, Phidias."

He had touched on a subject near and dear to her heart, Olympia's history and that of the Olympic Games in relation to Christianity. She ambled over to what had been the three-aisled basilica, which had been built of sandstone with later brickwork placed above it. She put her hand on one of the columns that had supported its wooden roof. It was warm and rough to her touch, but nice, real, something solid from a time long ago, which connected the early Christians of the land with the Christians of today. "I think it was the early Greeks' way of dedicating this land, and all that was good about the Olympic Games, to the God who had been made known to them by the apostles of Christ in the first days of Christianity."

He stood beside her, and his gaze traveled around what had obviously once been a beautiful church. It was the earliest and simplest type of church building. A rectangular central hall or nave was separated from side aisles by rows of columns. The building type had originated in antiquity as an assembly hall—a basilica.

"The Greeks certainly made sure to do that with the first modern Olympics held in Athens in 1896," he said. "There can be no doubt in anybody's mind who both the athletes and the organizers were honoring during those historic games."

She smiled, impressed by his knowledge. "Opening day was on Easter Monday—Bright Monday—the day after Easter. Easter is the most holy day in Greece, even more so than Christmas, so that was as loud a proclamation as any that the Hellenic planners could give as to Whom the games were intended to honor."

"The day after Easter. . ." he murmured, and even though she didn't know him well, she could tell that that day held a special significance for him. She suspected from the way the corners of his eyes seemed to turn downward, a sad one too. He shrugged, visibly trying to rid himself of some memory. "I'm sorry. My wife miscarried our child—a little boy—on that day many years ago. I can never think about it without melancholy seeming to grab ahold of me."

Her heart went out to him, and she understood then that she'd been right when she thought she'd detected a wistful sadness when she mentioned Natalia and Noel's baby a few minutes earlier. "You have nothing for which to apologize. That is one of the hardest things a couple can go through." Mamma had miscarried a child. Every year on the anniversary of the babe's birth—and death—they had all gone to the cemetery. Her parents had always told her how much they regretted never having had the opportunity to get to know that child and that that was something they were looking forward to doing in heaven. The fact that they had six other children made no difference to the loss of that one. Except in terms of having been blessed to have had other children, a family.

He nodded. "It was the closest my wife and I ever came to having marital problems. It had nothing to do with our love for one another, but everything to do with pain over the loss of our child. Really hard, especially since we were never blessed to have other children."

She could tell from the way his shoulders hunched that that was a grief that he still felt keenly. For him to mention it to her, a virtual stranger, proved how much it was still on his mind. She doubted that the loss of a child ever, even with the grace of God, left a person totally.

"It's something couples have a very hard time ever recovering from. Often marriages suffer because of it." That was the only time couples had almost broken up in Kastro. She had often been asked to be present when her father had counseled them, comforted them.

"And we weren't Christians then. We went through that tragedy alone, without our Lord to lean on. He was there of course; we just didn't know it, didn't know Him. Not in the full meaning of His being. Not with Him being the Lord of our lives."

She had thought he was a Christian. She'd seen him in church every Sunday since she'd moved to Ancient Olympia; it was something that seemed to be imprinted on the very fabric of his being—just as it should be with all Christians. She couldn't help how happy it made her to hear him declare it with words, though. She didn't pause to wonder why that should be.

"Did you ever consider adopting a child?" She had thanked God practically daily that her parents adopted Natalia. She knew that single women often adopted children today, but that wasn't something she had even thought about doing twenty-odd years earlier.

He breathed out deeply. "We were completing the paperwork on a young girl from Eastern Europe when my wife became ill." He shrugged and looked out around the site. "I would have liked to have brought her here. She's eighteen now. I've often wondered about where she's living and about the couple that was blessed to become her parents. I hope so much that she's happy."

"So." Martha paused and licked her lips, not really sure she should continue. This was a highly personal subject. But the way he looked at her, as if he needed to talk to someone about the children he'd loved and lost, compelled her to continue. "In truth, you've lost two children. Not just one."

When a poignant smile lifted the corners of his lips, she knew that she had been correct to speak. "You're a very perceptive woman, Martha. Most people don't realize how deeply I feel the loss of that little girl too."

"She was almost your child every bit as much as the baby your wife miscarried. Of course you miss her."

"How is it that you seem to understand? You said that you had never married, so I assume that you don't have any children." It was a statement, but a questioning one.

"Ah. . ." She smiled and bantered back. "But you don't know that for sure. As it happens, I do have a child."

A frown sliced across his forehead as a myriad of questioning emotions covered his face. Disappointment. Amazement. Gladness. It was as if he didn't know which one to settle on. She decided to enlighten him.

"When I was thirty-two, my parents found a newborn

baby in the bus station of the city close to our village."

"Found?"

She nodded. "Yes, they actually found an infant in a bus station. She had been abandoned there. To make a very long story short, since there wasn't a trace of the baby's biological parents, and no one claimed to have lost one, my parents adopted her, adopted our Natalia. But because my mother had just been diagnosed with a severe illness, the care of Natalia became mine. So in every way important, and even though we refer to one another as sisters, we're actually more like mother and daughter. I couldn't love a child of my own body more than I love Natalia. And even though I have never been blessed to share in the marriage relationship, as you were with your wife, God has blessed me in giving me a child to raise and love."

He whistled out through his teeth. "That is most definitely a testament to God's provision. He not only gave your sister a loving home but you, a child."

She thought about Natalia and the way her laughter—like crystal chiming in a gentle spring breeze—brightened all of their lives, and especially Mamma's during those ten years of her illness. It was because of Natalia that their mother had lived so long, because her mother had wanted to be with her youngest child for as long as humanly possible. "God is gracious. Like the saying goes, 'When God closes a door, He always opens a window.'"

He nodded, and she watched as he scanned his gaze out over the thoughtful valley and breathed in deeply of the sweet summer air. "Olympia is that window for me," he said after a moment. "I love living here. It makes me feel as if I can do anything. It's almost as if I am a young man again, free to dream and grow and do so much with my life."

"Umm, I know what you mean." She nodded and let her own gaze wander the tree-covered site full of historic stones, memories, and curious people from the world over.

Moving had been good for that reason too, and even though Kastro was beautiful at this time of year, there was something extra special about this valley she now called home. Although it was July and most of Greece was baking brown in the summer sun, the valley of Olympia was still green and fragrant.

"This outdoor church"—she motioned to the roofless one in which they still stood—"is one of my favorite thinking spots in the world."

"Thinking spots?" A smile brightened his features. "I like that." Then he motioned down to the white Bible that she held in her hand. "You must have a lot of Martha's sister, Mary, in you. Not only do you seem to know a lot about human nature, but also when I walked up, you were deeply engrossed in reading. And it's not the first time I've seen you sitting here doing so."

"You've seen me here before?" The question came out before reason could keep her from voicing it. She'd seen him around town, but never at the ancient site, a place she made a point to visit at least once a week.

He shrugged his broad shoulders. "You've always looked so thoughtful that I haven't wanted to bother you." A quick grin sliced across his face. "I couldn't help myself today."

"I'm glad," she admitted and thought that she would have stayed with her gaze fastened to his all evening long if the strong gusting wind hadn't chosen that moment to pick up the brim of her hat and nearly blow her straw bonnet off her head. "Oh, no," she exclaimed and laughed. Her hat would have left her head completely and traveled through the ruins of Olympia on its own if Leo hadn't placed his hand on top of her head and held it in place while she adjusted the silky scarf straps beneath her chin. "Thanks."

He smiled, and standing back so that she could precede him from what remained of the church building, he motioned toward the path that led to the exit. Except for the crunching sounds of their feet upon the earth, they walked in companionable silence. They passed the foundation of the huge temple of Zeus, then the Philippeion—a circular building offered by Philip of Macedonia from Northern Greece that honored his family, including his more famous son, Alexander, known as "the Great." The temple built to honor Zeus's wife, Hera, came next. It predated that built for Zeus, and in it, one of the more famous statues of antiquity, the Hermes of Praxiteles, had been found. Martha often went to the archeological museum of Olympia just to stand before that mighty work of art and gaze at it.

Beyond Hera's temple was the arched entranceway to the ancient stadium. Martha walked around the stadium practically every time she visited the site. While doing so, she liked to think about all the people throughout time who had participated in races there as well as those like her who walked, or ran, its course during modern times for their own personal reasons. The prototype of all stadiums in the world today, it was another of her thinking spots.

Looking to their west was the square-shaped palaestra—the building that had been both the wrestling school and living quarters for the athletes. Pine trees now grew where that magnificent edifice had stood. Standing, stoic columns in straight lines marked where its porches had been. Martha wondered if it was as enchanting when it had actually been a building as it was now.

They were heading up the section of the path flanked by trees when Leo asked, "So do you?"

She frowned and looked up at him. Had she missed something? "Do I what?"

"Do you have a lot of Mary in you? Do you like to study at the feet of Jesus?" he repeated the question he'd asked while still at the site of the church. She couldn't help but hear the hopeful quality in his voice.

Martha nodded. "My father is a Greek Orthodox priest, and he long ago taught me the love of studying the Bible."

"Really? An Orthodox priest? I have such a huge respect for that ancient tradition. It's so misunderstood by many people, mostly for lack of knowledge. And very often it's confused with Catholicism."

"When actually the Orthodox were the first to protest against some of the teachings of the Roman Catholic Church, centuries before Martin Luther. Martin Luther did not in any way protest against the Orthodox Church."

"That's right," he agreed. "And it's the trunk of Christianity forming a direct line back to Pentecost." He paused. "I'm actually surprised that you know about Martin Luther."

She sent him a mildly critical look. The implication behind his statement almost seemed absurd to her. "Of course I know about him. Next to the study of the Bible, my father always stressed church history, even relatively recent church history such as the Reformation." A smile touched the corners of her mouth in a bantering way. "On the contrary, it's your knowledge that's surprising."

He shrugged. "My wife was an avid history lover. And especially church history. She made sure I learned." He smiled. "I'd like to meet your father someday. He sounds like an interesting man. Very open-minded."

"He is."

"And I can even speak to him in Greek." Using careful diction he said, *"Milao Elinika*—I speak Greek."

Martha stopped walking and swiveled to look directly at him. She knew that her mouth had dropped open. "You speak Greek?" How rare was that? Much of the English language might have been derived from Greek, but it was still unusual for an American to tackle the Greek alphabet. Ancient Greek for scholarly reasons maybe, but rarely did people try to learn modern Greek. The expression, "it's all Greek to me," wasn't coined because of Greek's simplicity.

He nodded, and she could tell that he was proud to admit that he did. "When I realized, six years ago—shortly after my wife died—that God was leading me to Ancient Olympia to make my home, I started learning it."

"That would have been about the same time that I started studying English formally and"—she looked at him and that connection she had sensed between them seemed to sizzle faster—"when I, too, was being led to Ancient Olympia."

"Amazing to think that God was moving in our hearts about this place at the same time."

four

But as Martha continued to walk down the path with Leo at her side, she didn't think that *amazing* was the word. More like *miraculous*, especially when she considered her father's longtime prayer for her: that someday a wonderful man would come into her life with whom she would experience the joys of marriage.

Could this be the man? Could Leo Jones be the one God has marked out for me since the beginning of time?

With the same surety that had made her certain that no man had been "hers" before, she was almost certain that Leo was that man now. It was all very strange. It made her feel almost out of control. What was it her father had said? To let God lead her down the new path her life was taking, even if the steps seemed uneven at times? She couldn't ever remember her steps feeling more uneven.

Martha believed in the power of prayer—especially her father's prayers—and she didn't believe in coincidence. Ever since her father had told her his prayer for her life, she somehow knew that God would bring a special man into it. Like a treasured secret, it was something she almost expected.

But now that the man her father had been praying for seemed to be before her—next to her!—she wasn't quite sure what to do about it, about her feelings for him. She had always thought she would jump at the chance to marry the right man. But now she didn't know if she really wanted such a change in her life, something especially strange since she was so attracted to this man.

Martha didn't like conflict. Her life ran smoothly and that was the way she liked it. A romance would be nice—especially with this handsome, articulate, Christian man—but she would have to think very carefully about anything more. She would only take a further step if she was certain that it came from God, that she could join her life with Leo's without creating problems in either of their lives by doing so.

She slightly shook her head. Her thoughts were moving in her mind like a runaway horse on a racetrack. She had only just started talking to the man an hour ago. But because of her father's strange confession two months earlier, she was already thinking in terms of marriage. That was too quick. Even for her.

"How long have you lived here?" she asked, wanting to rein in her thoughts and get them back on track.

"Only about two months."

She looked at him. "Same as me, then." Her voice was little more than a whisper. "And are you going to live here indefinitely?" She wasn't sure where that question had come from, but Martha didn't want to live anywhere other than Ancient Olympia. If he didn't plan on living here forever, then that would put an end to any relationship they might have even before it started.

"God willing."

Yes, God willing. She looked straight ahead. In the end that's what everything came down to. She had to remember that. And trust. Trust God. "Where did you live in America?" she asked, wanting to get away from her deeper, confusing thoughts.

"Olympia."

Her brows shot up, like *Baba*'s did when he was confounded.

"Olympia, Washington. It's the state's capital city," he explained.

Martha shook her head. "I had no idea that there was a city named Olympia in America."

"You'd be surprised at the number of 'Greek' cities to be found there," he said, flashing her that full smile of his. "We even have an Athens in the state of Georgia." He grimaced. "Unfortunately the reproduction of the Parthenon is located in another state, in Tennessee. But my Olympia"—he patted his chest—"was named for the Olympic mountain range that runs along the Pacific Coast to the north of the city. I assume that those majestic mountains were in turn named for Mount Olympus in northern Greece, which is how this area"—he waved his arms out—"received its name, too, in honor of the mythological gods who lived on Mount Olympus. At least that's what my mother always told me, which was nice to think about. It always reminded us of where at least part of our family's heritage came from."

His family's heritage? Now she better understood his choice of Ancient Olympia as his home. "From here?"

He nodded. "My grandfather on my mother's side."

She touched her fingers to her lips. "My mother's family too."

"Are you serious? You mean, we"—he moved his hand back and forth between them—"could be relatives?"

She waved her hand in a circular motion, which in Greek indicated the passing of time or an event. "Way back."

"Yes, way back," he agreed just as they arrived at the exit to the ancient site, and they stopped walking and turned to face one another. "Well, Martha—"

"Martha-Mary," she informed him.

"What?"

"Since you like Lazarus's sisters so much, I think I should tell you that my entire Christian name is Martha-Mary. My parents wanted me to embody the characteristics of both those famous Bible women so they gave me both of their names."

He shook his head. "Have you heard about the book *What's in a Name?*"

Had she heard about it? Since Noel, Natalia's husband, was its author she had an autographed copy sitting on the shelf behind the cash register in her shop. She even sold the book. But Leo was too new an acquaintance to let him know about her famous brother-in-law, or her sister, for that matter. "Yes."

"Then you will know that the writer shows how important it is to find the correct name for a person. Your father did that for you."

"Do you really think you know me well enough to conclude that?" she couldn't help asking. Forthrightness had always been her way.

"Well. . ." He surprised her by taking her hands in his and looking down at them. She was astonished with herself for letting him and even more at how perfect it seemed. "From your hands, which have the look of your having used them well during your life, I know that you are not idle." Her face grew hot, and she would have snatched her hands back, but from the timbre in his voice, she knew that he hadn't meant his words unkindly.

"Beautiful hands," he whispered, justifying her thoughts. "Helping hands of character, of love." He rubbed his fingertips over her shaped, but shortly cut, nails and up her fingers, past her knuckles, to the backs of her hands. He didn't let go of them when his gaze returned to her face. "And from your sitting on a bench beside a church building that was built in late antiquity reading your Bible, I know that you are definitely a Mary."

In spite of her reservations, her heart was beating to its new romantic tune even as she quickly spoke. "The truth is, until recently the Martha side of me was stronger than the Mary side." Even with a shop to run, coming to Olympia had freed a great deal of time for Martha to be Mary. She had quickly learned that running a home for a family was much more work than taking care of a business. The business had working hours. A home didn't.

The sun had lowered in the sky, and in the light of its red rays, she watched as a slow, very manly, very sweet smile spread across Leo's face. "Martha-Mary, you are a woman I hope to meet often in my travels around Olympia. Both the ancient site and the modern town."

She couldn't move her gaze away from his. Found that she didn't even want to.

For this man, this most remarkable and attractive man, was looking at her just as she had seen Noel look at Natalia, *Baba* at her mother, Stavros at Allie, and as so many other men had looked at their mates in Kastro, in New York, in churches everywhere, and while shopping in her store. Martha had never been envious of any of them. But having felt that special emotion of having a man think she was so unique as to warrant that valued look, Martha knew that she could never go back to not wanting it, not needing it.

Dear Lord. Is this the one my father has been praying would come into my life? He's like. . .a fairy prince. And even though I don't know how far I really want our relationship to go, I know right now that just as I must draw breath into my lungs and my heart must beat, I must get to know him. But how? Show me the correct way, Lord.

"Where can we next meet?" she heard him ask and blinked at how he seemed to answer her prayer with his question.

"Once Upon a Time. . ." The name of her shop automatically passed over her lips.

His smile deepened. His fingers softly stroked the backs of her hands, and with the happy sounds of tourists that surrounded them fading into the background, and with a blackbird chirping out a sweet tune in the plane tree beside them, he spoke softly, affectionately, in a dreamy sort of way. "Once Upon a Time. . .in a land far, far away. . .that time had almost forgotten. . .there lived a lovely woman full of grace and beauty named Martha-Mary—"

She giggled, breaking the spell, and when he stopped speaking she could have kicked herself.

But when the slow, secure smile of a man who didn't embarrass easily spread across his face, she knew that everything was all right. "I'm sorry." She licked her lips. "I like how your story goes, but—"

"Our story," he corrected her, and she almost forgot to breathe, as the world seemed to stop revolving on its axis and stand still. Her world, anyway.

" 'Our story'?" she squeaked out.

"The story I hope might be ours," he returned, and her heart pounded against her chest with the force of thunder in the sky, but she had never felt better. "You interrupted me before I got to that part."

"I'd like that," she admitted and felt just like the heroine in a romance novel, but an inspirational one now where the heroine wasn't fighting the normal progression of a love plotted out by God. "But to have our own story, in order for our story not to end here, we must, as you said, be sure to meet again. Soon."

"Soon. Now that's something I like."

Martha was glad that he obviously liked to do things as rapidly as she. Once she made up her mind about something, that was it. And she had made up her mind that in spite of any reservations she might harbor, about unwanted changes and conflicts he might bring to her life, she wanted to know Leo Jones better. She had never thought in terms of romance as going fast, but she knew that to go slow wasn't in her makeup, evidently, not even where romance was concerned. Then again, she had lived for nearly fifty-seven years on God's planet without a close relationship with a man. How slow was that? She just wouldn't tell Natalia how quickly she let a man into her heart, not after all her own warnings to her sister. "I was just telling you the name of my shop, where we might meet next time." At his confused look she explained. "Once Upon A Time, that's its name."

As if a light flipped on inside him, his eyes widened. "That store on the main street of Olympia that is always filled to overflowing with women is your shop?"

She nodded. "Once Upon A Time. . ." She giggled. Giggled again. She hadn't giggled. . .ever. But neither had she ever had such a conversation with a man as she had shared with this one for the past hour or so. "You must always come by when my Needlepoint Ladies are there."

"Needlepoint Ladies?"

She nodded and explained. "Three times a week a group of ladies come with whatever handiwork they are doing, and we all work together. Since needlepoint is my specialty, that's what the gathering first started out as. But so many of the ladies are masters at so many crafts. Some crochet, others knit, others carve, while still others paint. One lady hand paints beads, while an octogenarian even paints authentic

Byzantine icons. And if the ladies so desire, Once Upon A Time sells what they make. For some, it has become a good source of much-needed income."

A whistle passed his lips. "And you have only lived here for two months?" he asked rhetorically and squeezed her hands, reminding her only then that he still held them firmly in his grasp. It had felt so right, so normal, so comfortable even, that she hadn't noticed. "I've often passed your shop and thought that it must be one of the oldest, most established in town. It's always full. You must have quite a good head for business."

She had to suppress the pleased smile that wanted to erupt at his praise. It delighted her in a way no one else's had. "That has come as a bit of a shock to me too." Once Upon A Time was doing so well that she knew that she had to look for someone to help her run it during the busy summer months. She closed every Sunday—the reason she was able to be out now—but she was finding that keeping store hours six days a week was a bit restrictive and too much for one person to handle. Especially since the shop was often busy.

"What's your secret?"

Giving his hands a light squeeze, she let go of them, and crossing the country road, walked over to the bus stop on the opposite side. He followed beside her. "Well, I only sell the best quality of handmade folk art and crafts that I can find. But mostly, I treat the shop like it's my home and welcome everyone who walks in as if they are my honored guest. Because they are. I feel as if everyone who comes into the shop is coming to spend a few minutes of his or her life with me. That's special."

"No, Martha-Mary, I think you're the special one," he muttered thickly.

She didn't know what to say. To have him look at her as if

he thought she were the most wonderful, most unique, woman in the world was one thing. But for him to say it was something entirely different. It brought everything onto a level that she wasn't sure she was prepared to reach. They might have seen one another for the previous two months, but they had only just met. To cover her confusion she fiddled with the straps of her purse and was relieved when the bus pulled up. "Are you riding back to town?" she asked and heard a breathless quality to her voice that almost made her cringe.

"No. I have my bike." He motioned in the direction of the fancy bike on which she had often seen him riding. It was chained to a tree. He smiled, obviously not put off by the change in her manner. "I will drop by Once Upon A Time tomorrow, if that is okay with you."

She nodded and smiled, but really felt like yipping for joy. By then she should have control of the emotions that were bouncing around in her like Ping-Pong balls in perpetual movement. "Tomorrow," she agreed, and as she climbed the three steps onto the bus and sat down, she only hoped that it was a promise.

She closed her eyes. Her blood sang through her veins as she remembered his words. *"Once Upon a Time. . .in a land far, far away. . .that time had almost forgotten. . .there lived a lovely woman full of grace and beauty named Martha-Mary. . ."*

She opened her eyes and looked out over the historic valley as the bus wended its way down the road. She wondered how their story might end.

A part of her hoped it might be "And they lived happily ever after. . .in a land far, far away. . . ."

But another part of her was still confused, and she didn't know what she hoped for—strange for a woman who was normally so well acquainted with her own mind. Even though her father had been praying for a mate for her, and even though a part of her thrilled to the idea, she knew that at this point in her life, to join her world with that of a man's was a major life change. Everything would have to be perfect in order for her to do so.

But oh, how she liked that tall, slender man. She placed her hand upon her chest, and as she took a deep settling breath, she reminded herself again to do what she had done all her fifty-six years.

As with everything else in her life, she would leave any relationship with Leo Jones up to God. She would follow His leading.

A secret smile played with Martha's lips.

And Leo's leading, of course.

five

Leo walked toward the bushes at the side of the road and stood in the protection of a family of blossoming laurel, which hid him from the eyes of the many tourists now exiting the ancient site. He watched as the blue bus drove down the fragrant country road toward the town of Ancient Olympia, its next stop.

"Dear Lord," he whispered out on a breath of yearning. "Is it because of this woman, this very special woman named Martha-Mary, that you have directed my steps here, to the town?" he asked, and a montage of the times he had seen Martha around town immediately flashed through his mind.

The picture of decorum and fine taste, Martha had always been elegantly dressed. But more than her fine clothes and nicely coifed hair that softly brushed her chin, it was the way in which she both held herself and in which she interacted with other people that most captured his attention. She might have only lived in Olympia for two months, but to Leo it seemed as if she had been a pillar of the town for decades.

But more than her outward beauty, it was that of her soul, her spirit, her intellect, that so moved him. She was a salt-of-the-earth woman with sparkling eyes and an intelligence that ran deep. But it was that immortal part of her, which her lovely body housed, that most affected him.

She seemed to personify the verses found in the final chapter of Proverbs. " 'A wife of noble character who can find?' " he softly recited a few lines into the summer's eve. " 'She is worth far more than rubies. . . She is clothed with strength and dignity. . . She speaks with wisdom, and faithful instruction is on her tongue.' " He paused and, knowing that Martha-Mary was indeed the reason he had been led to Olympia, breathed out with a thankful heart, "She couldn't be better, Lord. Thank You."

Leo felt the same exhilaration shoot through his system as when he had been a young man of nineteen and in love for the first time. It was an all-encompassing feeling, one that reached to the farthest parts of his body to tingle it with anticipation, and to the innermost part of his being where his spirit and soul danced together at the thought of a mate, a companion, a woman, to call his own once again.

Leo was ready for love. He had yearned for another woman—a wife—to share his life with since the day he had let Susan go, about two years after she had died.

It seemed unbelievable that during the first time of really talking to Martha—of speaking more than just a few words of greeting—he should know that she was the one for him. But even more, that God should endorse the truth of his feeling within his soul, as God most definitely was still doing, in His still, soft way.

But he had been patient.

Leo grimaced at the self-righteous sound of that.

For the most part he had been patient. For the first two years after his wife had passed away, he hadn't dated at all because he hadn't wanted to, hadn't yet thought of himself as being wifeless, as being single again. He had immersed himself in the study of God's Word, his work, and in sports. In that order. The study of God's Word had been the greatest comfort to him in his loss. He knew from reading the wonderful words of promise and hope that the wife of his youth was safe even if he couldn't have a personal part in taking care of her any longer.

After two years, though, both wanting and needing a special woman with whom to travel through life, he had started dating again. He had gone out with many women. But from the first, he had somehow known that none were for him.

That thought caused a quizzical frown to slice across his face. So maybe it wasn't so incredible to recognize that a woman was the one for him during their first meeting. "Love at first sight?" he questioned himself. "More like love at first conversation."

But it had been the proverbial love at first sight with Susan, his wife. And even though they had wasted many years with the empty living monetary success often brings to couples, they had, before the end of their journey together, found the Truth that had set them free to be the people they were created to be in Christ Jesus. And then the love they had felt at first sight for one another became something many times more precious. It was one such as that ordained by God for His people, a glorious time of learning together with their spirits tuned to each other's because they were both, first and foremost, tuned to the God of all creation.

Leo took a deep breath and squinted up toward the sky, which was bathed in a summertime palette of orange, red, pink, and yellow. His gaze followed the little fork-tailed swallows that swooped and turned, dipped and dived, as they played tag in the foreground, while the sounds of their playing on the soft evening breeze brought delight to his ears.

Was he actually in love with a woman he had only just talked to? He was, he admitted to himself, and with the admission, his spirit felt as light and free as those playful birds. It was soaring along with them.

He laughed, a giant laugh that filled his brain with endorphins. Leaning toward the bush, he inhaled the fragrance that softly perfumed the air around the laurel. He knew that he would forever associate this sweet but mild bouquet with the discovery of his second love. Some might question the validity of his sudden decision as being made on the wings of emotions and, as such, one that shouldn't be trusted.

But Leo didn't.

He had always been quick to make decisions, to come to conclusions. Decisiveness was one of the traits that had made his software company one of the most successful and which had given him the freedom to move halfway around the globe and to run his company from wherever he chose.

He only hoped—especially now that he had talked to Martha-Mary and realized how much she meant to him—that he might be able to continue to do so. But there were situations with the company that might need his personal attention. He had always known there was a chance that he might have to move back to Olympia, Washington, and split his time between both Olympias. Until meeting Martha, he hadn't minded the idea. Now he did.

He sighed. He would cross that bridge when he came to it. Leo had learned long ago not to borrow tomorrow's possible problems today.

Leaving his hidden place among the shrubbery, he hummed a favorite tune as he strode over to his bicycle, where he had left it under the watchful eyes of the canteen owner.

He only hoped that he would be as successful with Martha-Mary Pappas as he had been with his business.

Somehow, he felt that he would be.

He strongly believed that God had ordained his steps to meet hers here in Olympia, starting six years earlier. Actually—he corrected his thought as he waved his thanks to the canteen owner and secured the bike chain around its seat—God had ordained their steps to walk together here in Olympia long, long before the original Olympic Games had started in 776 B.C. From the very beginning of time, even. . .

As he straddled the bike and clipped his helmet beneath his chin, he wondered how much more encouragement he needed than that to seek out and pursue, with an eye toward marriage, the lovely woman named Martha-Mary.

None, he thought, as he started cycling down the road, which the bus, holding the woman he loved, had passed over only moments before.

None at all. For when he decided upon something, he always achieved his goal. Always. And this was one he was certain God Himself had endorsed.

" 'Once Upon a Time. . .in a land far, far away. . .that time had almost forgotten,' " he softly recited the words he had spoken to Martha earlier, " 'there lived a lovely woman full of grace and beauty named Martha-Mary. . .' and. . .a man named Leo Jones who loved her. . ."

He laughed, a laugh unlike any that had sounded from him since his wife had died. Leo was genuinely happy.

And all because of a woman named Martha-Mary.

❧

The intercom buzzed.

Martha sat up in bed and opened her eyes wide, all at the same moment. Adrenaline from being awakened from a sound sleep pounded through her system like a wave from a choppy sea hitting the rocky shore. She glanced at Needlepoint. The buzz had only elicited a lazy lifting of one chocolate brown lid. Martha smiled at her blue-eyed feline friend as she placed her hand upon her chest to still her own heart's hammering. Throwing back the sheet, she slipped her feet into her sea-foam green slippers, grabbed her matching silk robe from the hook on the back of her bedroom door, and padded down the polished plank floor of the hallway to the living area of her apartment.

Her gaze went to the digital clock. 23:37.

By Greek standards, and especially during the summer months when most indulged in afternoon siestas, it wasn't considered too late. But Martha had been unusually tired after returning from her cousins' that evening and had gone straight to bed rather than watching TV while needlepointing, as was her normal custom during the final hours of the day. People who knew her well, though, would know that she was normally awake until well past midnight, so she was quite certain that someone she knew well must be at her door.

Would Leo, the man who had occupied much of her thoughts during the evening—she had been thinking about him even while carrying on conversations with her cousins— come to her home at this time of night? She hoped not. Since she'd only recently met him, that wouldn't be right. In fact, it would be a major minus against him. And she didn't want any negatives aligned with him.

As if scanning through a movie on her DVD player, she had gone over bits and pieces of their conversation all evening long. She had thought about the way his mouth moved while he talked and how it was always quick to stretch and fill in the smile lines that surrounded it. She had also thought about the way she felt when he had taken her hands in his.

His touch. . .

So perfect, as if her hand had been custom-made by the Master Designer to fit into his and none other. There had been nothing strange about it. But that was the most unusual thing of all. Never had it felt right to hold a man's hand. The few times she had dated, she had always been uncomfortably conscious of a man's hand around hers. She hadn't been with Leo. It had been as if it were an extension of her own. . .

But she knew it wouldn't be Leo at her door. She sensed enough about him to know that he wouldn't come to a woman's home uninvited at this time of night. Especially one he had only talked to for the first time that day.

Martha lifted the receiver to the video intercom, which enabled her to observe and speak with visitors at her downstairs door. She was taken aback to see the young woman whose face filled the screen. "Maria?"

"Yes, it's me, *Kyria* Martha," the young woman replied, referring to Martha with the respectful feminine title. She turned great big, sad eyes up to the camera. "May I come in, please?"

Even with the imperfect image through the tiny in-house screen, Martha could tell that her young friend was troubled. Very troubled. "Of course, *kali mou*—my dear," she replied as she simultaneously reached for the button to buzz the girl in. But as Martha heard the street-level door being opened, then closed, and heard Maria's soft footsteps upon the steep marble stairs, she questioned what could have brought Maria from medical school in Athens to Olympia, rather than to her father's home in Kastro.

Unless—and in spite of the heat of the night Martha shivered at the thought—she and Dimitri had broken up.

Martha opened the door wide in welcome, and Maria dropped her duffel bag. She immediately fell into Martha's arms, just as she had nine years earlier when Maria had been thirteen and her mother had just passed away. And as with then, sobs racked the slender girl's body. Martha was certain, even before Maria got the words out, that her suspicion was correct.

"Dimitri. . .he. . .broke up. . .with me," Maria cried out softly. Maria was never loud even when expressing grief. "I just couldn't return to Kastro for summer holiday. . .where everybody would"—she hiccuped, and Martha knew that silent tears must have been falling from the girl's eyes throughout her long bus trip from Athens—"feel sorry. . .for me." She hiccuped again. "And my father. . ."

She couldn't go on, but she didn't need to. Martha understood. Her father, Petros Petropoulos, had never approved of Maria's relationship with Dimitri. Primarily because he felt it was one his daughter pursued rather than Dimitri.

Martha gently guided the young woman into her living room and over to the floral brocade sofa. "Shh, there, there, you did well in coming here, Maria. You know that you are always welcome in my home for as long as you want to stay."

Maria squeezed Martha's hands in gratitude as the girl sank onto the sofa. She turned her dark, intense eyes up to Martha. "I feel just as I did when my mother. . ." She stopped speaking and patted her chest. "It's as if my heart is being ripped out again."

"No, *kali mou*." Martha gently took her hands in her own. "It's different." She had to be firm about that. A man not wanting to pursue a relationship with a woman was not anything near as traumatic as a young child losing a parent. And even more, Martha didn't want Maria to let this hurt rule her life as she had with her mother's death nine years before. "I'm sure that Dimitri must have a good reason for deciding as he did." Martha had nothing but the highest respect for Dimitri.

She was certain that he wouldn't intentionally hurt Maria. "He probably doesn't think that you have enough in common to live a life together."

"But. . .I love him!" Maria cried softly, with all the lifelong adoration she had felt for the young man in the throbbing sound.

Martha had always felt guilty for wanting Dimitri and her sister Natalia to get together, knowing how this young woman felt about the man. But Martha had agreed with Petros, Maria's father, and never felt that Maria and Dimitri made a good match.

But that wasn't what the heartbroken girl needed to hear right now.

Sitting next to her on the sofa, Martha wrapped her arms around the young woman and cradled her head upon her shoulder, just as she knew her mother Emily would have done had she still been alive.

Who would know at this moment that this crestfallen young woman was one of the finest physicians in the making? As well as being one of the strongest people Martha knew.

"I thought he was going to ask me to marry him," Maria moaned out after a few minutes. "We had even talked a few weeks earlier about how much we both wanted to have children while we're still young. I had no idea that he didn't mean with me," she said, her voice much weaker than its normal, sure tone. "We never fought," she continued, as if that proved that they were a perfect match.

Martha handed Maria a tissue from the box on the end table. Dimitri and Maria were both too quiet, too much alike. She could imagine them sitting together and studying. But not much else. Dimitri needed someone full of fun and laughter, a get-up-and-enjoy-life kind of girl—someone like

Natalia. While Maria needed a man who could show her that life was more than just one responsibility after another.

After Maria's mother had died, the young teenager had taken on the duty of raising her two younger brothers and sister. Not only had she raised them, she had been their teacher. Their father, full of grief and anger that no one had been able to save his wife and newborn baby, had deserted their nice home in the village and moved his four children to an old woodsmen cabin up on the mountains high above Kastro. Martha was certain that if it hadn't been for Allie, when she was the new doctor in the village, Maria's father probably never would have come down off his mountain. But Allie had proven to him that she was a doctor who cared and made him see that he was risking his other children's lives by staying up on the mountain far away from civilization and help. Moving back to the village had been perfect timing for Petros's other children, but for Maria, her responsible, staid personality had already been formed. And when she saw a grown-up Dimitri—an extremely fine-looking, impressive young man— her childhood attraction had formed, as well.

"I wanted to marry Dimitri. And soon. He would have married me if he had felt about me the way he did Natalia." Martha didn't hear even an iota of rancor in her tone. Maria had never faulted Natalia for Dimitri's love of her, especially since it was unrequited. Besides, Natalia loved Noel, not Dimitri.

"Attraction is a complicated thing," Martha finally replied. She was just beginning to realize that, since meeting Leo. That so-called chemistry that makes one person highly attracted to another was fine as long as both parties felt the same way, but misery if only one did. She was so thankful that Leo seemed to find her as nice as she found him.

"I know." Maria's lower lip jutted out just as it had when she had been a young girl. "I just wish I could have proclaimed. . .to the world. . .that Dimitri was *thekos mou andras*—my husband," she finished, as tears dropped from her eyes like rain from a heavy autumn sky.

"I know, *kali mou*, I know," Martha murmured and held her close.

But Martha's heart was breaking for her young friend, and she had to press her own eyes tightly shut to keep her own tears from falling. How she wished that things could have been different. If anyone deserved happiness, it was this young woman who had experienced too much pain in her twenty-two years.

Martha hoped and prayed that someone as bright and dazzling as a new and sunny summer day might soon come into Maria's life, someone who would make all the sorrow recede like the tide at the pull of the moon. Someone. . .

six

After another hour of tears, talks, and hugs, Maria finally fell asleep in Martha's spare bedroom.

Martha had just finished decorating the guest room the previous Friday. The walls were papered Easter blue, with little sprigs of welcoming jasmine. Fussy priscillas covered the inlaid windows. An antique rosewood dresser topped with an old-fashioned, silver-handled brush and comb set and a cut crystal vase filled with fragrant white roses sat against the large wall opposite the double bed.

It was a room meant to welcome visitors. Martha was only glad that Maria had come this week and not the prior one. The sleigh bed had been the last item to go in the room on Friday. Martha had made it up that same evening with eyelet sheets of snowy white, with a hand-crocheted summer throw that one of her needlepoint ladies had custom-made. The blanket was the exact same blue as the walls, and the pillows were Martha's own needlepoint designs of Siamese cats. She had her cat, Needlepoint, to sleep with every night. She wanted her guest to have, if not the comfort and soft, rhythmic breathing of a real cat close by, something similar.

Martha had the room ready in the hopes that she would soon have a visitor. She was glad that Maria was her first guest and that she had the lovely room waiting to offer. Maria needed the psychological security and warmth. Even in her weary and traumatized state, Martha had seen the relief jump into Maria's dark eyes when she had shown it to her. The room was just what the doctor ordered for the broken heart that ailed Maria.

As Martha lay in her own bed thinking about Maria's unexpected appearance, she knew that their midnight reunion had been a time of healing as well as one of decision. They had decided that Maria would spend not just the next few days as Maria had planned before returning to Kastro, but her entire summer break in Ancient Olympia. She would help Martha out at Once Upon A Time make some money, as well as take the time to sit back and get her bearings, to take stock of her life. Something the girl hadn't done. . .ever. She had gone from being mother to her brothers and sister to being a medical school student.

She needed a holiday from personal responsibility.

Was way past needing it, in Martha's opinion.

Martha reached over to the far side of her bed to pat Needlepoint good night. As she did, she thought about how Maria's life and her own were similar in that they had both cared for their father's family. But in Martha's case, she had been a woman of thirty-two when her mother had become ill and Natalia had joined their family, forty-two when her mother had succumbed to her illness. Maria had only been a child of thirteen, looking forward to a new member of the family joining them. Instead, both her mother and her infant sister had died.

Martha sighed. Leo's baby, like Maria's youngest sister, had died before even having the chance to draw a breath of his own.

She wondered how old Leo's son would have been now, had he lived.

Squeezing her eyes shut she whispered a prayer for Natalia and Noel's child, whose body was being woven together within the safety of Natalia's body. "Dear Lord, please bless Natalia with a safe and normal pregnancy. Please let her little baby be born healthy and strong." Martha was looking forward to the birth of that new little human with all the hope and excitement that any woman soon to become a grandmother might feel. She couldn't wait to hold Natalia's baby in her arms. She secretly hoped it might be girl, a little girl who looked just like Natalia.

But for right now, Martha knew as she lay back against her plush pillows, to the soft and comforting sound of her cat's content purr, that she enjoyed the opportunity of having Maria in her home and the chance to act as a surrogate mother to her. She knew that had the situation been reversed, Emily—who had been her dearest friend—would have done the same for Natalia.

Maria's arrival in Olympia couldn't have been better timed, either. Not only was the spare bedroom ready, now Martha didn't have to search for someone to help her with the shop. Having someone she knew well to rely upon was a huge relief. It would also give her the time to let the Mary part of herself continue to grow strong and to study the Word of God and learn.

But that thought easily reminded her of Leo and how he had brought up the Bible story about the sisters, Martha and Mary, after finding out her name.

Leo.

As she remembered their meeting earlier that day, a smile touched Martha's lips, right before a happy sigh—something similar to the sound her cat made when her purring turned into content breathing.

Martha could hardly wait for the new day to start so that she could see him again.

She glanced at her alarm clock. One-thirty.

It was the new day.

She closed her eyes. She wouldn't have much longer to wait. Or to sleep.

But even with the excitement thoughts about Leo brought to her, Martha fell asleep with a prayer on her lips for the young and hurting woman in the next room.

"Dear Lord, please heal Maria's heart. And Lord, if it be Your will, please bring a young man full of sunshine and fun into her life—one who will teach her how to live life joyfully. And a man who might help to make the memory of Dimitri fade like a favorite, but worn-out old shirt."

❧

The crystal chimes on the back of the shop door jingled late the following afternoon. Martha looked up from explaining the computerized cash register to Maria and into the deep green eyes of the man she had been waiting to see pass through her store's portal all day long.

"Leo," she gasped, not even thinking she should hide her pleasure in finally seeing him again. Her lack of pretense, however, was rewarded with the quick and full smile that she already associated with him as his long athletic gait took him across the polished plank floor.

Before Martha knew it, her hands were once again encompassed by his—a feeling that she thought most heavenly. Certainly not something she had ever experienced before. "Hello, Martha-Mary. It's been too long." His voice was husky.

She glanced at the antique clock on the wall behind his left shoulder. "Almost twenty-four hours." She could tell from the downward tilt of his head that her concurrence surprised him. "I had thought to see you sooner than this."

His left eyebrow rose slightly. "A complaint, Martha-Mary?"

Her smile grew. "Most definitely."

"Well, if I have to hear a complaint, at least it's one in which I am in complete agreement," he admitted wryly, then, with a serious tone, said, "I would have come sooner," his lowered voice leaving no doubt to the truth behind his words. "Actually, I had intended to be the first one through your door this morning"—his voice returned to normal—"but my housekeeper's sister went into premature labor." It was then that she noticed the strained look in his face. "I wanted to do whatever I could to assist the family."

"Of course." Martha saw the pain of losing his own child in the intensity of his eyes. "How are mother and child?"

"Fine, thankfully; this story has a happy ending." Unlike the unhappy one when he lost his own little child, Martha thought. "We managed to get the new mother to Patra before the babe was born. Having the correct facilities for preemies, the doctors there expect the baby to completely recover from the ordeal of being born too early."

Martha could feel the tension leave his body as he spoke the blessed words, their utterance seemingly needed to cement the reality of this new baby's health. "That's wonderful, Leo. I'm so glad."

He took a deep breath before letting it slowly slide out, and Martha suspected that the whole episode had cost him greatly in terms of personal memories. "Me too."

"Patra has very good facilities for premature babies." Maria spoke from their side in an encouraging way, and Martha turned to her with a smile.

"Leo, I'd like for you to meet Maria Petropoulos. She's from my village, Kastro, and is the daughter of two of my dearest friends. She's a medical school student, so she speaks with knowledge concerning Patra's hospital. And just last night"—Martha put her arm around the girl's shoulder and gave her a slight squeeze—"Maria agreed to stay with me through the summer to help me run the shop before heading back to med school in the fall."

"That's wonderful." Leo extended his hand. "How do you do, Maria?"

Maria reached for it. "Very well, thank you." She tilted her face toward Martha. "Since coming to stay with *Kyria* Martha-Mary." She put the emphasis on the name Mary, and Martha felt the blood rush to her face. No one but her father had ever called her by both her names. And he did so only on select occasions. Maria knew that, and from the speculative way in which her young friend was regarding her, Martha was sure that she also knew that something was up. Martha would explain everything to her later. Not that there was much to explain—as yet.

Her unexpected feelings for Leo confused Martha and ran the risk of throwing her perfect life into another orbit. But a big part of her—that innate part of every woman that wishes for a mate of her own—admitted to being hopeful that there might soon be more to tell. She was following her decision of the previous day and leaving her relationship with Leo up to God. It was one that had granted her peace beyond understanding.

Maria's next words, though, had her momentarily forgetting her romance with Leo.

"You're not the only one who has a name change, *Kyria* Martha-Mary," she said, and Martha frowned, wondering what she meant. "As of today—this very moment actually"—she flashed a quick smile that showed off her even teeth—"I have decided to start introducing myself as Stella."

"Stella!" It surprised Martha, but pleasantly so. That had been the name Emily had actually wanted to give her firstborn child. But wanting to follow Greek tradition and give the first female child the paternal grandmother's name, Emily had settled for Stella being her daughter's second name. But Stella was the name Emily had used when talking to her daughter. Stella, "Star" in Latin, had always been Emily's little star. She had always told her daughter to shine like the stars in the universe.

"I've missed my mother always calling me by that name," Maria—Stella—said, echoing Martha's thoughts.

Martha nodded. "Me too. . .Stella." It wouldn't take long to remember to call her that. It was more her name than Maria had ever been.

"Plus. . .because of. . .everything"—she waved her hand before her in an all-encompassing way that Martha knew meant Dimitri's splitting up with her—"along with spending the summer with you, I'd like to make another major change in my life."

"I think it's a good idea." Martha was surprised at just how much she liked it. Maria's use of her second name might help her to leave the somber Maria persona behind and recapture the happy, carefree girl she had been before her mother passed away.

"Well, Stella," Leo said, "I'm pleased to make your acquaintance, and I'm especially glad to learn you will be helping *Kyria* Martha-Mary out at Once Upon A Time. That will give her more free time to spend with me."

Martha tilted her head toward him. "I like the way that sounds."

Stella's big brown eyes widened so much that Martha thought her eyeballs might pop from their sockets. Martha laughed and winked at her young friend—an old signal between them that meant she would tell all later—then turned back to Leo. "Do you like the shop?" she asked.

While glancing around, Leo nodded approvingly. "It's one of the most wonderful stores I can ever remember having the pleasure of entering. So homey and yet exquisite too."

As if seeing it for the first time again, she let her gaze follow his around the various sections of the room—the wooden shelves and tables tastefully arrayed with exquisite handmade crafts as well as selective souvenirs from the ancient Olympic Games; white-washed walls covered with fine artwork; and the back right section of the store with its two cream-colored twill sofas situated around the arched arms of the huge fireplace, the place where she welcomed tired tourists to sit and rest and where her needlepoint ladies gathered. A sense of contentment filled her that she could agree with his assessment.

She listened as he continued. "Everything is set up like a museum piece, but it's approachable." His gaze met hers. "It's truly a 'Once Upon A Time' kind of place. It makes one feel all that is right and good in this world of ours."

"Thank you. That's just what I wanted to do." It pleased her immensely that that was the impression it gave him. "It's the culmination of many dreams of mine come true." She had loved setting the gift shop up, but she loved even more coming down the steps each morning, opening the shutters, and turning the sign on the door to read "Once Upon A Time is opened for all the people of the world who wish to enter."

"I feel as if I have stepped into another era," he commented.

Martha looked around at the beamed ceiling, the deep, recessed windows with their slated shutters, and the *tzaki*—the fireplace—that was the focal point of the living area. All was similar in her apartment upstairs, and she had to agree. "You can't imagine how thrilled I was when I learned that this traditional building, situated right here on the main street of Ancient Olympia, had been put on the market immediately after extensive renovations had been completed. The only thing I had to do was to unlock the door and move in."

"How old is it?"

"It was built in the late 1800s."

"That's pretty old."

She smiled. "By Greek standards, it's really not."

He chuckled. "You've got a point there."

She motioned toward the living area. "Would you like a cup of coffee or a glass of iced tea and maybe a piece of baklava?" She referred to one of the more famous Greek pastries. Made of walnuts and honey and layers of paper-thin pastry dough called philo, it was a sweet for which Martha was well known. One of her specialties.

"May I take a rain check?"

"Of course." Martha spoke the words but couldn't help the cold fingers of embarrassed disappointment that seemed to move over her skin like a cloud over the sun. She hadn't realized until that moment just how much she'd been looking forward to sitting right now and getting to know Leo better. A form of sadness that that didn't seem to be his desire unexpectedly flooded her.

What was wrong with her? She had never imagined such a feeling could be hers from a man speaking such a simple sentence. She didn't seem to know her own mind any longer, a very unusual occurrence. Is that what love did to a person? If it was, she wasn't so sure she wanted it.

Leave it up to God, a voice inside her reminded. *Follow your practice of a lifetime, and leave Leo and your feelings for him and how those feelings might change your life in God's capable hands.*

Yes. That was what she would do. She was glad for the diversion that a large number of happy, carefree tourists entering the store at that moment afforded. She smiled at them to hide her regret and embarrassment.

"What I had hoped—" Leo said, and as she turned her face back to his, she tried not to let the hope she felt at his words be too evident. He motioned out the door at the mellow softness, which the sun riding closer to the horizon cast upon the land. Gone was the brash plunder of its hot draining rays when at its zenith. It was as if the earth sighed at the respite that the sun traveling westward on its daily journey afforded it—a good night's sleep was ahead, but first, a glorious, Grecian summer's eve. "It's such a splendid evening, I had hoped that you might like to take a stroll with me," he suggested and turned to Stella. "That is, if Stella thinks she can handle the store on her own for awhile."

"No problem," Stella said quickly, and Martha smiled at her. Could Stella possibly know how grateful she was for her answer and her presence? Just having the younger woman close at this most unusual and remarkable time in her life was a security Martha hadn't even realized she needed. Until living it. But she knew Someone else did know what she needed. That was another reason why He had sent Stella to her. She—and her confusion—needed Stella just as much as Stella needed her.

"Are you sure, *kali mou?* This is your first day after all."

Stella motioned to the cash register. "I've got it down now, but"—she handed the cell phone to Martha—"to ease your mind and mine, take this. If I need anything, I'll call you." She winked as she came from behind the table that served as the shop's counter on her way to help the tourists. "Have a great time."

seven

Martha and Leo did indeed have a great time—so much so that they started taking evening walks on a daily basis. Sometimes they wandered around the tree-lined streets of the modern town of Ancient Olympia, stopping now and again to enjoy an ice-cream sundae at an outdoor café under the cool, whispering leaves of a reaching plane tree. Other evenings they meandered the fragrant country roads surrounding Olympia. Other times they went into the archaeological site itself and envisioned how it must have looked nearly two and a half millennia earlier at its heyday, when it was one of the greatest places in the world.

Martha decided to enjoy the here and now with Leo and to stop thinking about how their future might unfold. But it was something she had to continually turn over to God. She was too confused by both wanting a future with him and not wanting one that might upset her careful life. So far there didn't seem to be any major conflicts that might disturb their relationship. But even though the idea of joining her life with a man's was enough for her to consider, she refused to give in to temptation. She continually gave her fears to God and let Him guide her in her relationship with Leo. Totally.

A few days after their first walk, they took a break from roving the ancient site and sat on their favorite fallen column, the one where they had first talked. Leo said, "The ancients didn't consider Olympia a city, rather, a sacred precinct."

Martha nodded her agreement and gazed over the pastoral

valley with all its beautiful trees—evergreen oaks, Aleppo pines, planes, poplars, cypresses, and ever-present olive trees—tucked between two rivers, with the conical and green Mount Kronos climbing to the north. "I can well understand how people who didn't have God's Word in their heart could believe this place to be sacred. I guess they felt close to 'God,'"as they perceived supreme beings to be. Especially when considering that verse in Romans and God's invisible qualities."

" 'For since the creation of the world God's invisible qualities— his eternal power and divine nature—have been clearly seen, being understood from what has been made, so that men are without excuse,' " he recited. Shifting his gaze to her, he seemed to watch her expression closely. "Is that the one you mean?"

She nodded.

A frown pulled his dark brows together.

"What?"

He took a deep breath. "Personally, Martha, I think that verse refers to God's general revelation to mankind—that of the creation, the natural world, and its natural law—and should have actually directed the ancient people toward Him, especially considering their historic capacity as a race to think, and not to images made to look like mortal men." He pointed to the right toward the ruins of the temple to Zeus. Only the three-level base and huge, fallen drums of circular-cut stones remained now, but it was still easy to see how massive and grand the structure had been. "Phidias's gold and ivory statue of Zeus sat in there."

"True." She pointed toward what had been the church. "And that's where Phidias sculpted that statue in about 435 B.C.—

it was the site of his workshop before the church was built there. In the fifth century A.D., the statue was transferred to Constantinople where it most likely perished in a fire about forty years later. That early Christian church was built on the ruins of Phidias's workshop, and even though the church building itself has suffered at the hands of invading humans and nature and it's in ruins today, too, the message that it brought to this land, unlike the one the temple to Zeus purported, is not.

"The people of the first centuries after Christ who lived here, upon being given God's special revelation—His Word—combined it with His general revelation and left their questioning, pagan ways and built churches to honor the God of Jesus Christ, the God whom they had loosely worshipped before as the Unknown God. Once they understood who He was"—she flashed him a grin—"and it was that delight in reason, in thinking, you mentioned a moment before that assisted the Greeks, they built church buildings, successors to that one there." She nodded toward the brick walls with its arched windows and the marble screen of Byzantine workmanship that remained of the structure. "And the church has been in their hearts for much, much longer than that statue of Zeus, made of gold and ivory—elements of God's earth—sat in that temple. It's not something that can ever be burned in a city fire or"—she indicated the entire area that had sat under water for centuries due to the Alpheos River having changed its course in the Middle Ages—"destroyed by floods or earthquakes, Vandals, or thieves."

His chest lifted on a deep breath and slowly went down. "In the fifteenth chapter of John, twenty-second verse, Jesus said to His disciples concerning the nation into which He was born—the Jewish nation—'If I had not come and spoken to them, they would not be guilty of sin. Now, however, they have no excuse for their sin.'" He sighed. "The Jews not only had God's Son, with them but they had received God's special revelation in the Old Testament. And yet so many rejected Jesus. Many didn't—enough to start the infant church—but still, many did."

He paused, and Martha watched as his glance slid over the ruins of the church building and stopped on the crosses, which were cut into the marble screen. "The Greeks didn't reject Christ. Even though they had a culture that was one of the greatest the world had ever seen, or will ever see, they didn't hold on to their own pagan ways, but recognizing a better Way, embraced it."

His gaze left the church and turned to her. Martha's heart seemed to soar with the swallows that played in the wind. How similar in thought she and Leo were! It was a heady experience, almost the same as when they held hands.

She knew that he hadn't agreed with her at first, and yet he had listened and honestly considered her words. He had done that many times during their time together, something very important to any future relationship they might have. The physical attraction that sizzled between them was wonderful, but thoughts, feelings, and beliefs would eventually render that shallow. She had to know that she could always speak her mind with Leo and that he would always carefully consider her feelings. And vice versa. Agreement about everything—except for their belief in Christ—wasn't the issue. Communication was. "That's the way I see it, Leo."

He looked down at her hand and rubbed his thumb across her knuckles before training his gaze back to hers. "You know, when I told my friends at my church in America that I was moving here, to Ancient Olympia, many of them had questions about the Olympic Games and Christianity."

"It's an interesting subject and actually something that I've given a great deal of thought to." She had. Both the ancient and modern games. She knew that some people thought that the games should never have been reinstated. But she had always thought that a little study about it would change most minds. Even devout Christian minds.

"Tell me," he encouraged.

Nodding, she motioned to the historic land that surrounded them. "What the ancient Greeks did here with the original Olympic Games was not perfect." The Games had been held in honor of Zeus. "But it was something that brought the people together for the promotion of the brotherhood of mankind, and it was a way to take the bellicose nature of man and place it not on a battlefield, but rather in a sports stadium in a movement of peace. They did it for more than a thousand years, practically every four years." She laughed gently. "We people of modern days who have both God's special as well as His general revelation have only held the Games for a little over a hundred years. And that includes missing three modern Olympiads due to the two world wars in the twentieth century."

"You have given this subject some thought, haven't you?" he said, with a lazy gleam in his deep eyes that made the blood rush to her face.

She held her hands up to her checks. "When I get on the subject of the ancient games compared to the modern ones, not to mention God's involvement in it all, I do tend to go on so."

"No." He lowered her hands from her face, then squeezed them while staring at her in that deep intense way that made her feel like she was the most special woman in the world. The depth in his eyes held all the sparkling adoration that a woman could ever hope to see in a man's gaze. The multitude of green shades reminded her of this valley. His eyes were peaceful, calm, and intelligent, as if, like this land, they had much to tell. "I like it," he said. "I could listen to you talk all day long." He laughed. "Besides, I asked."

"Are you sure?" She laughed wryly. "Believe me, I have much more to say on the subject. I think it has always appealed to me because one of my ancestors—from all accounts a very strong Christian too—gave a great deal of support and money toward organizing the first modern Olympics in 1896. She attended them too."

He whistled between his teeth. "Really? I've never met anyone with a relative who attended the first games."

"I'm not sure if you've noticed, but I have a photo of that ancestor—Sophia—on the mantel at the store."

He nodded. "I wondered who that was. She was a very attractive young woman."

Martha had always admired Sophia and often regretted that her mother's relatives had lost virtually all contact with her after Sophia moved to America. Nodding, she leaned toward him and in a conspiratorial way said, "It gets even better. She met her husband at those first games. He was an American from Princeton, New Jersey."

"No kidding?" A smile played with the corners of his mouth. "So others in your family have been brought together by something to do with Olympia and the Olympic Games?"

"Others?" She frowned. "I don't know actually. But I imagine it's possible. Actually, I think Sophia and Henri's daughter married a man whom she met at the Lake Placid Winter Games in 1932. I don't know for sure, though, because we've lost track of the relatives from that branch of the—"

"No." He interrupted her. "Darling Martha-Mary, by others

I mean us." He flicked his pointing finger between them. Just a little gesture but one that said so much, that they were a couple. Martha's heart experienced that funny little jump it had so often done since meeting Leo.

"Us?" she squeaked, her voice unrecognizable to her ears.

The lines around his mouth filled with his smile. His head lowered toward hers, so close that the musky scent of his fine aftershave mixed with that of his own essence to fill all that was feminine in her. She felt such joy in being in his presence that she thought she must be dreaming. It was a form of intoxication, a good one, that God had decreed right and excellent between a man and a woman.

She closed her eyes to drink in the exotic moment, one serenaded by nature's orchestra—cicadas grinding, pigeons cooing, bees buzzing, and a warm summer breeze that played the leaves of the poplar trees into violins fluttering. But nothing in her life had prepared her for how she felt when Leo's lips—his perfect, sweet, masculine lips—touched lightly, like the wings of a butterfly—upon her own.

She heard a groan.

Was it he or she?

She wasn't sure. All she knew was that this was a moment she had never experienced.

"Darling Martha-Mary," he whispered.

She wished she could contain the small giggle, but she couldn't.

"What?" He chuckled in return, resting his forehead against her own.

"Don't feel bad, and please don't stop calling me by both my names, but. . ."

She paused and chewed on her lower lip. How she wished

she hadn't laughed. She would have much preferred to still feel his lips upon her own. Instead, there was the chance that she had offended him.

"Go on," he prompted with laughter in his voice, reassuring her that he hadn't taken offence.

"Well, I always feel. . .a bit. . .like a nun in a movie I once saw—I can't remember its name—when you use both my names."

The glint of humor in his eyes was a match to that in his voice. "Is that how you feel right now?" he challenged. Most people would call his deep, soft voice sexy, but she thought it made her feel like the most cherished woman in the world.

"No, Leo," she hastily assured him. "A nun is the last thing I feel like."

He stared at her deeply, as if he were trying to look past her eyes to see into her soul. His eyes narrowed more until he spoke the words Martha had long since ceased expecting to hear a man say to her. "*S'agapo*, Martha. I love you."

And just as when he had taken her hand in his, and when he'd kissed her, the words seemed natural and right. She didn't allow reason, which might question whether it was right for her life and his; she only whispered her feelings back. "*S'agapo*, Leo."

"You do?" He blinked as if he hadn't expected that reply, as if it were almost too easy.

She shook her head. "Darling Leo. What's not to love?" That was the truth. She loved everything about this man. The way he treated her, the way they talked together, laughed together. The way they believed the same things. But mostly, the way he made her feel. Special. Cared for. Loved.

"It's not too fast for you?"

"I like doing things fast. Besides, I'm just telling you that I find you the most wonderful man I have ever met. And you make my heart beat in a way that it has never done before." She put her hand on his forearm, relishing the feel of the muscles beneath his skin, the soft hair beneath her touch. "There's plenty of time for anything more." And she knew that that was the truth too.

"Martha, I believe that God brought us together so that we might share a future."

She knew he felt that way. She had sensed it from the first day they talked. It was one of the reasons she'd felt apprehensive about her life changing with meeting him.

Oh, it was so confusing.

She both wanted him in her life—embraced the idea of the wonderful change he would bring to her world, one God recommended for men and women—and yet, at the same time, she loved her life just the way it was. She loved living in Ancient Olympia, loved her shop, her apartment, her friends, her church. As much as it depended on her, she didn't want conflict of any sort in her life.

But whether she wanted it or not, it was there, because more than any of the things she loved about her life, she loved having Leo in it now. But in spite of her father's prayer for her, she felt that that very love might conflict with the good life she had made for herself in Ancient Olympia.

"I don't know about any future we might share yet, Leo." She spoke softly not wanting to hurt him—never that—but knowing that she had to be honest. "But I do know that I'm so glad that God brought you to this land that is so far, far away from the world but, so close to me."

"Oh, Martha," he murmured. And just before his lips joined with hers again he whispered, "Me too."

Martha wished that life might always be just as it was at this moment, wonderful and, as yet, so free of complications. But something—maybe having lived life for more than half a century—warned her that that would not always be the case.

eight

A few days later—days of shared joy in their new love for one another—Martha and Leo stood in front of the huge statue of Hermes of Praxiteles at the archaeological museum. Made of Parian marble—the fine, white marble found on the Greek island of Paros—and standing tall above their heads, it was the ideal combination of grace and strength that the sculptor, Praxiteles, had been able to form from an element of God's earth. The Olympian serenity on Hermes' face, as well as its perfect proportions, combined to make it one of the finest pieces of artwork in existence in the world. Its white marble was perfectly offset by the deep red of the walls behind it.

"We have this beautiful piece, and it's the star of the museum," she said as they walked through the cavernous halls of the museum toward the exit. "But it just makes me wonder about all the other works of art that the vulgarities of time have destroyed here at Olympia."

"We wouldn't even have it or all these other statues"—he pointed to those that lined the walls of the room they now walked through—"if the Alpheios River hadn't changed course, flooded the site, and hidden them from both the eyes of ravaging humans and other even more destructive elements of nature."

"Amazing to think of a flood protecting something."

"Even more is that a volcano can do that," he said. They passed the modeled reconstruction of the ancient site—which depicted the buildings of the ancient city in all their Hellenic splendor—and exited the museum. "Like what happened at Pompeii in Italy when Vesuvius erupted in A.D. 79."

She nodded her agreement, and threading her arm through his, they started down the tree-lined path toward the main road. Walking arm in arm in companionable silence was one of those nice little unexpected things that had come from her relationship with Leo. As silly as it might sound, it was something she really enjoyed about having him in her life. He was her man to reach out and touch, to hold hands with, to fix down his windblown hair. Little no nonsenses, those simple things were, nonetheless, what made both life and the new love they shared together special and oh, so romantic. No words were necessary to fill empty places because there were no vacant spots in their time together. Silence was time shared and golden.

As their feet crunched over the stones, the symphony of summer—the cicadas' drone, birds playing in the breeze, the sounds of children and their parents out together to inspect a bit of history—all played around them. Martha's mind wandered.

She had learned some very interesting things about Leo earlier that day. Her Needlepoint Ladies had met at the shop, and several had told her how Leo was known to fill any need in town he heard about. She knew that he often did handy work around the homes of the elderly who could no longer do the work themselves, but what she hadn't known was that he would pay plumbers and carpenters if the work was beyond his abilities. And he would do the same for young mothers who needed help. He would not only arrange for baby-sitters and housekeepers but pay their salaries too. Any injured or stranded tourist he heard about was always put up in a nice hotel, again at Leo's expense. He was, in essence, a silent "need meeter" around the town of Ancient Olympia. Although he asked all whom he helped not to tell anyone, Ancient Olympia was too small for it to be kept silent. Many other wonderful additions had come to town since Leo arrived—park benches, playground equipment for the children's park, equipment for the medical station in town.

She knew that he spent several hours every day running his American-based software business from his computer at his home office and that he often said he had business around town to take care of, but she hadn't known the extent of his endeavors until the ladies told her.

They had confirmed her suspicions that Leo's main business was people. Together with the priest in town, and a few others, he filled any and every need that he could. He was a good steward with both his skills and his money.

She squeezed his arm tighter against her own, and when he looked down at her, she smiled up at him. This man was becoming better and better with everything she learned about him.

"Tomorrow is my birthday," he said, out of the blue.

Coming to a full and sudden stop, she asked for confirmation that her ears hadn't deceived her. "What did you say?"

"That. . .tomorrow is my birthday." His brows came together, forming a solid line of question. Tilting his head he asked, "What's so remarkable about that?" He chuckled. "We each have one."

Martha touched her hand to her chest. "Yes, but, Leo, not normally a shared one. You see. . .tomorrow is my birthday too."

A wide grin split across his face. "Are you serious?"

She laughed. "Believe me, after celebrating fifty-six of them—fifty-seven as of tomorrow—I should know."

He made an amazed sound and ran his fingers through his thick hair before holding up his hand. "Wait a minute. Tomorrow is your fifty-seventh birthday?"

She grimaced. "Did you think I was older or younger?" Most put her about ten years younger. A vanity she admitted to because it had never been important to her. But was it important to Leo? Had he thought her younger, and was he disappointed to learn that she wasn't? Fingers of apprehension slithered up her backbone, and she scrunched her eyes together as the seconds added up.

Seeming to understand how far he had placed his proverbial foot into his mouth by his delay, he quickly replied. "No. No. You look younger. At least ten years younger. But your age isn't consequential to me, nor to my feelings for you."

Relief flooded her. That was the best thing he could have said.

"What I can't believe is I will be celebrating my fifty-seventh birthday tomorrow too."

She blinked, then opened her eyes wide. She knew that her father would have told her that her eyeballs were about ready to pop out of their sockets and run off to play basketball. "You mean, we not only share the same date, but we were born the same year as well?"

"It's seems that way."

She giggled. "I don't believe it. Natalia and Noel share the same day. But not the same year. I thought that was incredible. But this is even more so. I feel like a little kid with a secret treasure."

"I was going to ask if you would come out to dinner with me tomorrow night to help me celebrate, but I know that your family probably—"

"I'd love to."

"But what about your family?"

"In Greece birthdays aren't that big of an occasion. It's our name day that is celebrated grandly, with relatives and friends."

"That's right," he replied thoughtfully. "The name of the Christian saint in whose remembrance you were named."

She nodded. "I have my choice of either Martha or Mary since they are both Christian names, but because St. Mary's day—Maria—is a national holiday here on the scale of Thanksgiving in America, I celebrate my name day, then, on August fifteenth. That's in a few weeks. My father will be back from America, so he will come here, along with several other friends from Kastro, to celebrate it with me. I hope you will come to my party too."

"Hmm. . ." He twisted his head as if considering. "To not only meet your father but a good many of your friends at the same time. . ."

"And don't forget my relatives here in Olympia too." She slanted her eyes at him. "Does it make you nervous?"

He leaned down, drew her close to him, and lightly placed his lips upon hers before whispering, "I think I can handle it."

She had no doubt that he could.

His dark eyes seemed to drink in the essence of her. "But tomorrow you will be all mine." His low voice made her feel as if she were melting on the inside. "I know of a lovely restaurant on the sea where I can order a romantic sunset unlike any you have ever seen. So dress in your finest, and let's go celebrate the day of our birth."

She liked the way that sounded.

❧

The phone rang at Martha's apartment all morning long with

well wishes for her birthday. Her father and Natalia had been the first to call, all the way from New York and just before her father had retired for the night: Midnight in New York was seven A.M. in Ancient Olympia. The time difference never failed to amaze her father. He wished her *Hronia Polla*—Many Years—and asked her to describe the sunrise over the mountains near his hometown. Martha had gladly obliged, describing it just as Homer did in *The Odyssey*, "rosy fingers" and all. She had just closed the door behind Stella, who was on her way to open the shop, when the phone rang for the umpteenth time.

It was Dimitri. Martha had hoped he would call. She wanted to ask him a few things, needed reassurance about others. After the normal salutations and well wishes she did so, and his answers proved to her that she was right to think so highly of him.

"What I don't understand, Dimitri, is why you didn't tell Stella months ago, years even, that she wasn't the one for you. It's been very hard for her."

"Stella?"

Martha explained the name change—with which Dimitri wholeheartedly agreed—then he answered her question.

"If a woman loves a man, and the man feels much affection for her, isn't it worth trying to see if love can become a two-way pattern? I feel for Maria—Stella—many forms of love, *Kyria* Martha. All of those described by Paul in First Corinthians. That's why I tried. I thought that the love of friendship I have always had for her could eventually turn into romantic love. But it hasn't, and I know now that it never will."

Martha could hear the regret in his deep voice. "I just don't love her in the way a man should love a woman whom he wishes to marry," he said. "I know because I have loved in that way."

Martha knew he referred to Natalia, but she didn't say anything.

"It would be unfair of me to offer Stella anything less than that wonderful, romantic, storybook love she both craves and deserves."

"But isn't so-called romantic love the reason so many are divorced today?" *Am I asking for Stella or for myself? I most definitely share a romantic love with Leo.*

"Not if their love is, first and foremost, based on God's love."

My many talks about God-related things with Leo and our prayer time together have proven that Leo and I most definitely share that.

"As long as God is part of their union," Dimitri continued, "then romantic love can move on to the pure love—the agape love—which is the love of God in their lives. And then if all the loves talked about in Corinthians come into play in a relationship, it's the most perfect form of romantic love."

Martha knew that she had always liked Dimitri. Even as a child he had been wise beyond his years. So different from his parents, who had always let their emotions rule their lives. More than ever her heart ached for Stella. She could easily understand why the young woman was so enamored of this man, who was as handsome on the inside as he was on the outside.

"Even though there is a difference between romantic and physical love, it's when people start and stop at those two forms that there are so many divorces in the Western world today," he said. "People have forgotten about the spiritual side of their union and how that must be ordained by God. They have forgotten too that once a person gets married, all of the words on love in First Corinthians must be applied to their relationship even more."

"And—if you don't mind my asking—what sort of love do

you lack toward Stella? You don't find her attractive?" Martha couldn't believe she was being so bold. But she had to ensure that she was correct in advising Stella in the manner in which she had—to let Dimitri go.

"Maria—Stella, I mean—is a very attractive and desirable woman. To have a physical relationship with her would be a very easy thing to do, if she were that sort of woman and I, that kind of man. But I want more than that and for Stella too. I want the romance." He paused. "When I love I want to feel toward a woman like Solomon felt toward his wife. 'Place me like a seal over your heart, like a seal on your arm; for love is as strong as death. . . . It burns like blazing fire, like a mighty flame. Many waters cannot quench love; rivers cannot wash it away.'"

Martha's heart now ached for this intense young man. He had felt all that for Natalia. But Natalia hadn't felt it for him, but rather, for Noel. "I pray, Dimitri," she whispered, "that you will one day soon feel that kind of love for a young woman, one who will return it in kind."

He sighed. "Except that I would love to have a whole house full of kids while I'm young, I don't mind waiting. Like you, *Kyria* Martha, singleness is not something that rests badly on my shoulders. I do hope to someday find a woman to love, but until then, I will use the time wisely." He let out a deep sigh. "I just want Stella to be happy. I do love her—as a friend—and I hurt when I think of her hurting."

"Someday, she'll thank you for caring enough to let her go."

"I hope so, *Kyria* Martha. I hope so. Because to let go of what she was offering was one of the hardest things I've ever had to do."

That was something Martha, because of her relationship with Leo, could well believe.

nine

A few minutes later, Martha walked through the back door of the shop and, out of habit, checked to see who was there. The only patron was a young man with sandy blond hair, who looked over the hand-painted porcelain beads. Martha had never seen him before. As if sensing her gaze, he looked up and smiled warmly, as if he had a jolly laugh ready to erupt. Martha immediately liked the young man.

A smile formed on her lips, and she was about to ask if he needed help with anything when Stella sang out, *"Hronia Polla, Kyria* Martha!" Stella embraced her in a great, big hug.

Martha laughed and knew that she had to be beaming from all the love Stella had showered upon her since she awoke that morning. First, three fragrant yellow roses had been placed artistically on her bedside table for her to see upon opening her eyes, then a beautiful breakfast—complete with sterling silver and bone china, homemade bread and jam—set on the veranda awaited. Now this sunny greeting. As she turned to Stella, Martha felt certain that no mother could have felt more love from a daughter than she had from her friend Emily's little Stella, her Star. Even though she had been so unhappy lately, Stella had made a point to be cheery. Martha was very touched.

"Thank you, Stella. It's not even nine-thirty in the morning, but you've already made my birthday so special."

"It's your birthday?" the young man asked from behind

her. When she turned and nodded, he immediately said, "Happy birthday!"

"Why, thank you." Martha was touched that a stranger should care enough to wish her birthday greetings. She smiled at Stella, but was surprised to see that the girl had lowered her head and seemed to be busy with some papers on the desk. Odd. Stella normally enjoyed talking with the patrons.

"I like birthdays." The young man laughed. "All holidays, actually," he qualified and looked toward Stella's bent head. "Anything that marks a day as being special." He glanced back at Martha. "As indeed every day is."

"I couldn't agree more," Martha replied and slanted her gaze toward Stella, still perplexed that she seemed to deliberately avoid talking to the young man. Martha quickly turned back and asked, "Have you been in Olympia long?"

"About two weeks."

"Really?" That surprised Martha. She had thought he was just a short-term tourist, perhaps a recent high school graduate touring Europe.

He waved his arm in the direction of the ancient site. "I'm an archaeologist researching aspects of the ancient games for my dissertation."

Freckles sprinkled like grain across his nose, and his fine, sandy blond hair fell straight down his forehead. That and his compact size made him appear hardly old enough to be out of high school, much less in graduate school. "An archaeologist? You're in the right place, then."

That ready smile spread across his face. "Don't I know it. It's great here. Really special."

"I agree." Martha said. She liked this young man more and more the longer she talked to him. And the subject of his dissertation seemed fascinating. "How long will you be here?"

"The rest of the summer."

Stella lifted her head, and his gaze flicked to hers. "There's a chance I might be in Athens after that." Martha couldn't help but notice from the gleam of interest shining in his bright eyes, that in spite of Stella's quiet manner, the young man was enamored of her.

She wondered if the young man might be exactly the proverbial doctor-prescribed medicine for Stella. What better way for a heart to mend than to have an attractive, personable man show an interest? This young man was the total opposite of Dimitri, which would probably help too. Where Dimitri was tall, dark, and classically handsome—all the mystery of a deep velvet night—this man was like a field of wheat shining in the summer sun.

The chimes on the door rang. Martha turned, and from behind a bouquet of a dozen red roses, Leo's deep voice said, "Special delivery for Martha Pappas!"

"Leo!" Martha hurried across the room to meet him. Taking the flowers, she cradled them in her arms, while rising on her toes to receive his kiss.

"Happy birthday, Birthday Girl!"

"Happy birthday back to you, Leo."

"Happy Birthday, Leo," Stella sang out.

"Wait a minute," she heard the young man speak from behind them. Martha turned just in time to see Stella lower her eyes again. "It's both of your birthdays today?"

Leo nodded and placed his arm around her waist. Martha reveled in that feeling of belonging as Leo responded, "But it gets even better. We were born the exact same year too."

"Wow! That's neat!" The young man beamed at them, and Martha could tell he was impressed by the coincidence. "Happy birthday to you both."

"Thanks." Leo smiled down at Martha before turning back to the young man. "You're American?"

"Yep. From Pennsylvania. Philadelphia." He turned back to Stella, and Martha couldn't help but admire his persistence. "The City of Brotherly Love, which was named after one of the seven churches of Revelation."

Stella's eyelids moved slightly up and down as she regarded him, and Martha could tell that his knowledge of both ancient Greek and the Bible impressed her. "That's right."

Leo's eyes met hers briefly. He saw that something was going on between Stella and the stranger. Winking at her conspiratorially, he extended his hand to him. "I'm Leo Jones." He turned to Martha. "This is the owner of Once Upon A Time, Martha Pappas." After the young man's polite nod of greeting to her, Leo turned to Stella. "And this is Stella Petropoulos."

The young man walked toward her with his hand outstretched. Stella had no choice but to take it. "Stella means 'Star' in Latin and Petropoulos, well, let me see"—he tilted his sandy head and seemed to consider it, all the while holding Stella's hand—"*Petro* is for 'Peter' or 'Rock,' while the second part of your name, *opoulos*, means that you come from this area of Greece, the Peloponnese."

"That's right," Stella agreed, and as if suddenly realizing that her hand was still within his, she quickly let go and dipped her head shyly.

Martha and Leo's gazes met briefly before Martha asked, "And you are?"

"Brian." He flashed a self-conscious grin before divulging

his last name. "Brian Darling."

Martha returned his smile. Of course he was. He couldn't be named anything other than Darling. She pointed at the autographed copy of Noel's book, *What's In a Name?* and sent a smiling glance at Leo. She had given Leo a copy when she'd told him all about Noel and Natalia. "My brother-in-law wrote that book," she said to Brian Darling. "I think he would like your name."

Brian laughed, exactly the infectious laughter Martha had expected him to have, which made his blue eyes sparkle and dance above the freckles covering his nose. She glanced at Stella. She was looking at him as if she were trying to figure him out. "He certainly would. Especially if he were to meet my sisters. They are so. . .cute. . .and well. . .darling." Martha couldn't help but wonder if he had looked in the mirror lately. But she didn't say that. Most men didn't want to be called "darling," except by the woman they loved.

From the way Brian Darling's eyes returned repeatedly to Stella's face, Martha was sure he wouldn't mind Stella's calling him that way. But in order to have that happen, Stella would have to leave her love of Dimitri behind. She wondered if Brian would be patient enough to wait for that to happen. Martha hoped he would. She wasn't sure, of course—only time would tell—but Brian seemed to have exactly the personality Stella needed in a man. From the way Brian looked at Stella, Martha suspected that some interesting days were ahead.

Martha wasn't above helping him. She motioned toward the living area of the store and offered Brian a pastry in honor of the day.

"Baklava!" His bright laugher filled the four corners of the large room in answer to Martha's invitation. "Are you kidding? I'd have to be crazy to say no." But Martha could tell that what he liked most was the chance to sit with Stella and get to know her.

Brian, Leo, and she started toward the sitting area, but when Stella's attention returned to the cash register and she claimed she had work to do, the frustration on Brian's face, which was as open in happiness as it was in disappointment, almost hurt. But the three of them had a nice time, even though Brian's gaze frequently wandered toward Stella. After he left, Martha and Leo agreed that he was a fine young man.

While Leo went to put the flowers in a vase, Martha took the chance to question Stella. "Why didn't you come and sit with us? Nothing is so pressing that you couldn't have taken a few minutes. Brian seems like such a nice young man."

"Almost too nice," Stella murmured.

Martha frowned. "What do you mean?"

Stella set down her pen and gave Martha her full attention. "*Kyria* Martha, I still love Dimitri. It's too soon for me to. . ." She paused and shrugged. "I don't know." A heavy sigh escaped her. "Brian does seem like a very nice man. I'm sorry for that comment. But it's too soon for me to think about. . .anyone else. . .yet," she said, rubbing her fingers over her eyes.

"Where shall I put the vase?" Leo interrupted, and Martha, detecting a bit of moisture in Stella's eyes, walked toward Leo, to give Stella the privacy to control her emotions. She felt bad, though. Her young friend was still hurting so deeply. Dear Lord, Martha breathed out a prayer, please give me both the right words to speak to Stella, as well as presenting me with just the right time to do so. Martha knew that timing in talking with a young person was just as important as the words.

Stella's heart had to be open to any words she might say.

"Oh, Leo, the flowers are beautiful." They were a work of art, God's work. She took a deep sniff of the bouquet. The whole room seemed to fill with their sweetness. "Put them on the table in front of the sofa, I think." She motioned to the large couch where she and Leo had just been sitting adjacent to Brian, who had been on the smaller love seat.

He placed the cut crystal vase, then, coming back to Martha, drew her into an embrace and whispered into her ear the hour that he would pick her up for their date that evening.

"Our date," she answered back and, feeling bold, planted a quick kiss upon his lips. "I like the way that sounds."

"Me too," he said.

After sending Stella a quick wave, Martha walked with him to the door. She watched him walk down the main street of town until he turned the corner and was out of sight. Then she returned to the cash register and Stella.

"You're so lucky, *Kyria* Martha," Stella said softly. Martha turned to her in question. What was she lucky about? "To have found such a man," Stella explained, and Martha smiled her agreement. Although she didn't consider herself lucky so much as blessed. "Leo is so romantic and loves you so much." Martha heard the wistful quality in her voice and knew then that what Dimitri had told her on the phone about Stella's need for romance was absolutely correct. She admired Dimitri even more for realizing that he couldn't give it to her.

"You will have a romance someday soon."

"Soon?" Stella asked, turning her head to stare at the wall. But Martha was certain she wasn't seeing the paintings or afghans artfully arrayed below on a vintage truck, but rather the love for which she so yearned. "Do you really think so?"

If the way Brian had looked at Stella was anything to go by, Martha thought it would be a lot sooner than Stella imagined. "Just be open to God's leading, Stella. Be open to whom He might bring into your life."

Stella's shoulders sagged. "That's the problem. I've associated myself with Dimitri for so long that I just can't see myself with anyone else," she said, confirming Martha's thoughts on why her young friend seemed so shy around Brian. He wasn't Dimitri, and any man who showed an interest in her would make her feel uncomfortable because of that.

Martha rubbed her hand between the girl's slender shoulder blades and spoke as softly as she could to take the sting out of her words, "But, Stella, Dimitri isn't yours. And he never will be. If you want marriage someday—"

"I do!"

"Then you have to face that it will not be to Dimitri, but rather to a man who will be much, much better for you. One of God's choosing and not your own."

"God's choosing," Stella repeated, and a smile touched the corners of her lips. With the first flicker of hope Martha had seen in her eyes since she had come to Olympia, she said, "I kind of like the way that sounds."

ten

Martha left Once Upon A Time earlier than usual, to ready herself for her birthday date with Leo. She had made an appointment with her hairdresser to lightly trim, highlight, and style her hair. Its chin-length razor cut now softly swept her cheekbones as she walked home, and when she ran up the twenty-two marble steps to her front door, it bounced. A reflection of Martha's mood. Martha had her hair professionally cared for every week. It was another thing she had started upon moving to Ancient Olympia and a life change that had made her feel good about herself. Special. She never worried about her roots showing or it growing to an awkward length.

Long massaging soaks in her pink, marble Jacuzzi were more luxuries she started after moving into her own home in Olympia. The only structural change to her apartment she made when moving in was to the master bathroom. She had had it designed by the same interior designer responsible for Natalia's well-appointed Fifth Avenue apartment in New York City. Until visiting Natalia in New York, Martha hadn't even realized that bathrooms could be so luxurious. It was her favorite room now. Hanging furs, a shelf elegantly arrayed with her collection of antique perfume bottles, a skylight, and a stereo system that normally played Vivaldi's *Four Seasons*, helped to make the room with its plush carpet of pink rose so special. After soaking in the apothecary's personal blend of basil and lemon essential oils, and being massaged by the water jets for half an hour, Martha patted herself dry with a thick, soft bath towel. Leaving the bathroom, she went to inspect the contents of her walk-in closet.

Natalia had sent her several outfits from New York the previous week, and Martha knew she would wear one tonight. She wanted something previously unworn for this evening, an outfit that she would forever associate with her first birthday dinner with Leo. And she knew what she wanted when her gaze fell upon the knee-length skirt with a striped diagonal pattern of black and yellow. They would be dining outside at a classy restaurant overlooking the Ionian Sea. The huge, yellow summer sun would give way to the black silky night. The skirt would go well with the ambience of nature, and the fitted, pale yellow, short-sleeved sweater of silk and cashmere blend would in turn go with the skirt. She was certain Natalia had chosen it to be a match.

Martha dressed, then stood in front of her cheval mirror to critically observe what Leo would be looking at all evening, a purely feminine desire to please the man she loved.

She turned to the right, then to the left. Although she was on the short side, her figure hadn't changed much in the last twenty-five years. She was still slim with youthful curves. It had been a bit of a shock when she had started donning designer clothes to discover just how well she could wear them. She pressed her hand against her tummy, sucked it in, then smiled at the reflection of Needlepoint, who yawned from her corner of the bed behind her.

"Hey." Martha turned to the cat. "You don't have to look so bored. I'm not too bad for a fifty seven year old," she said and walked to the cat to scratch her under her chin. A deep, contented purr answered her.

Giving her cat one last pat, Martha returned to her closet and slipped her feet into a pair of black leather thongs. She looked with longing at the Manolo Blahnik, two-inch-heeled sandals that sat beside them. Natalia had sent them to go along with the outfit. But high heels were the only fashion items in which Martha didn't indulge. She was too afraid of falling and breaking a leg. Spraining it, at the very least. And that was something she couldn't afford to do. Not with Once Upon A Time to run. The flat thongs would have to do.

She reached for the thick gold-cuff bracelet Natalia had sent to her in celebration of this day last year and the black, ruched leather clutch. She added money, lipstick, tissues, and a comb inside, snapped it shut, and glanced at her reflection in the mirror now that her ensemble was complete.

She might not be twenty-five, but it sure wasn't visible in the way her pulse beat, her spirit soared, and her face beamed. She was going out on a date with the man she loved. You didn't have to be twenty-five to feel that anticipation, that excitement.

As the doorbell buzzed Leo's arrival, she turned away from the mirror feeling like the most blessed woman in the world.

‌ ❧

That feeling only escalated when she opened her front door to Leo, and they stood for a minute, unabashedly taking in one another's appearance. Dressed in a tailored linen jacket, matching slacks, and an Italian silk tie with the fleur-de-lis emblem of the city of Florence elegantly printed upon it, he looked as if he had just stepped out of a boardroom.

That thought surprised her.

He had always been so casually dressed before, athletically attired or in blue jeans or shorts and a polo shirt, that she had always associated him with being just that: a casual man who, because of the wonders of the computer age, was able to carry out his business from his home here in Greece as easily as he did from the States. But attired this way, it was as if she were seeing another side of him—one similar to the high-powered men in suits who walked the streets of New York—and one that he wore as comfortably as he did casual clothes. He oozed innate power, and she realized that she really didn't know too much about what he had done—about his business in general—before moving to Ancient Olympia. He had said that he had a software company. For the first time she wondered what, exactly, that meant. His lean cheeks were freshly shaven, revealing the natural lines of his features, all angles and strength; there was nothing weak about his face. She somehow knew too that that was a reflection of who he was.

But when he smiled, that half smile full of lazy confidence that she was so familiar with, she forgot everything but who he had been to her during the previous weeks—a warm and giving, caring man that made her world shine in a way it had never done before. Because of Leo, getting out of bed in the mornings was an adventure. She counted the moments until he either walked through the doors of Once Upon A Time or called her on the phone with a merry good morning. She wished life could go on like this forever, with nothing to change just what they shared now. She treasured each moment and had to continually give her fear—that something or someone or some situation would eventually change it—over to God.

She watched as the lazy gleam turned into that of a man who was very pleased by what he beheld. It sent her pulse skyrocketing. And when he pulled a fragrant bouquet of pink roses framed by baby's breath out from behind his back, she instinctively held out her arms for them. "Oh, Leo," she cradled them close to her and closed her eyes as the aroma filled the air around them. "More beautiful flowers for me. Thank you." They were such a lovely birthday present, and along with the ones he had given her that morning in the shop, she would carefully dry each one as a keepsake.

"They aren't half as beautiful as you, my darling," he said, and placing his hands on her shoulders, he leaned toward her and slowly lowered his lips to meet hers. Their smooth warmth moved softly, lovingly, a dance that was like flowers blowing in a spring breeze. "Happy birthday, Martha," he whispered, after a moment, letting his hands slide to her neck and up to cup her face.

"Happy birthday, Leo," she whispered back, and turning her head, she kissed the palm of his hand.

He pulled her close to him and, heedless of the flowers between them, whispered, "You smell so good, feel so perfect. I love you, Darling. So much."

"As I. . ." She inhaled the manly musk that clung to his freshly shaven cheeks, and she couldn't speak as a storm of sensations engulfed her—the aroma, the awareness, the essence of him. Their birthday celebration could end right here, and it would still be the best ever.

"As you. . . ," he prompted, after a long moment. With his thumb he traced the exposed column of her neck, sending little shivers of longing coursing through her system. Tilting her head back, she looked into his eyes. They had darkened to the deepness of an olive-tree grove at dusk. But still, as with the underside of an olive leaf, his eyes sparkled and gleamed silvery. The leaves did so when touched by the sun, his eyes from the light that was within his soul.

When she could finally answer, her voice sounded as foreign as the wondrous feeling that had become a part of her since meeting Leo. "As I love you. . ." She didn't know where their love would take them, only that it was the truth. She loved him. Dearly and more and more with each day that passed.

He sighed deeply, satisfied. He held her, giving them both the chance to regain their equilibrium, one that they knew as mature adults and as children of God they must recapture. Then Leo stood back and, using more willpower than she knew she had, moved his gaze away from hers and swept it around her living room before he focused back on her.

"This is the first time that I've been in your apartment," he said, glancing around the room once again. She wondered how he saw the parquet floor; lacy curtains fluttering at the windows, *tzaki*, and the feminine print of her floral sofas.

"It's lovely. So similar in feeling to Once Upon A Time. . ."

She was pleased that he sensed that. Part of her dream had been to always make her shop seem like her home. She reached for her clutch and the decorative bag that contained Leo's birthday present, a needlepointof the ancient church at the archaeological site that she had both designed and stitched. Leo opened the door and motioned for her to go out first. He closed the door behind them and held out his arm. She threaded hers through his, finding great pleasure in the feel of his lean strength through the fine linen of his summer jacket. They walked down the steep stairs together.

The whimsical thought went through her brain that with Leo's arm to lean on, she could have worn her high-heeled sandals after all.

eleven

The Bay of St. Andreas sparkled as though thousands of shining diamonds had been tossed upon it as the setting sun highlighted the softly rolling sea. The wind blew Martha's hair along her neck in a feathery caress that was almost as sweet as Leo's hand upon it had been earlier. A happy sigh escaped her, and Leo chuckled.

"You look like a content cat."

"Well, since, as you know, I'm partial to cats, I will take that as a compliment."

"And here's another one. You're lovely. As lovely in a human way"—he motioned out to the water—"as that setting sun is upon the bay."

Martha sighed. "You really must love me."

Leo chuckled low in his throat. "Ah. . .there's no doubt about that, darling Martha-Mary. And I hope to be celebrating every one of our birthdays together in the future."

Martha's breath caught. If they were to do that, they would have to go through life together. It was almost too wonderful to consider, but at the same time, too much to consider. Even though she would like to marry Leo, she knew that much needed to be discussed first. This was not something that could be agreed upon lightly. Their romance had been wonderful, but marriage was more than romance. It was also facing the hard realities of life together on a daily basis.

But that wasn't for tonight. Tonight was for fairy tales and fun. "I hope so too, Leo," she whispered. "Happy birthday." They had exchanged the wish many times during the evening; they were still like children in their wonder of its simultaneous occurrence.

He reached for her hand. "It really is one of the best ever."

"The best ever for me," she specified but didn't mind that he couldn't say the same. He had been married to a woman he'd loved very much, and she would be happy with it being "one of the best." She never wanted to take anything away from his life with Susan. It made her happy somehow to know that he had been happily married before. That meant that he had been a success as a husband, and in a world permeated by divorce and short-term relationships, that was very special.

"I love it here. I think it's one of my favorite places."

She looked at him quizzically. "Do you like it more than Ancient Olympia?"

"No. Ancient Olympia is my very favorite place and where I choose to make my home. But this is definitely beautiful." A lazy smile crossed his face. "Maybe it's because it's connected to Olympia in that it was the ancient port of Pheia, where the ships from around the Hellenic world brought contestants, diplomats, spectators, and others for the ancient games. It's probably the reason I like it more than any other seaside location."

He motioned toward a low-lying home sprawled atop the north-side bluff of the horseshoe bay. "Now that's quite a location in which to live. I'm sure that the people who call that home think this bay is the best place in the world."

"We do," a woman said from the table behind.

Martha and Leo turned to see an attractive woman taking a squirming infant from her husband's arms. The woman smiled as she bounced the fractious baby on her lap and motioned to the house on the bluff. "I'm sorry to interrupt, but that's our home, and it is the most special place in the world. To us at least."

Her husband smiled over at her. "That it is."

"From here it looks like a Shangri-La," Martha commented.

The woman smiled. "Although not hidden from the world like that imaginary land, it is our utopia." She motioned to her husband and the rest of her family, which included a boy of about eight, a girl of about six, as well as the baby she held in her arms.

"You're American?" Leo asked.

"I am," the woman replied. "My husband was born and raised here in Greece but lived in the States for many years."

"But we all live there now." The husband motioned at the sprawling house. "I'm Luke, and this is my wife, Melissa. And these are our children."

"I'm Leo and this is Martha."

"Nice to meet you both. Would you like to join us for coffee?" Luke offered. He chuckled, tickling the tummy of the infant, who wiggled like a worm. "If you don't mind our little one. She's teething and gets a bit out of sorts around this time of day."

At the encouraging look Martha sent his way, Leo quickly accepted. "That would be wonderful." He motioned toward the squirming baby, who was as cute as she was fussy. "But only if I can have a turn at trying to calm her."

Melissa and Luke turned startled gazes at one another. But their faces didn't begin to compare with how Martha felt.

"You can try, Leo. But she's pretty finicky about who she lets get near her. Especially when teething," Melissa warned.

"I love babies," Leo returned. "And funnily enough, they normally like me, too, and, even better, quiet down when I hold them."

He and Martha pulled their chairs over, and Melissa handed him a cloth diaper to drape over his shoulder. "Let's see if the charm still works," he said, as he placed the baby against his shoulder and, with the tips of two fingers, rubbed her little back in a circular motion.

When she gave one final sputter, then stopped fighting and fidgeting, everyone at the table stared at him with their mouths hanging open.

"She's quiet," the boy, who Martha thought was the image of his father, exclaimed. "She's actually quiet."

Luke chuckled. "You've got to teach me that trick."

Melissa turned to Martha and asked, "How many children do you have?"

Martha felt the blood rush to her face. She quickly waved her hand between Leo and herself. "We're not married."

Seeming to sense how uncomfortable she felt, Leo quickly continued, "I'm a widower, and my wife and I were never blessed to have children. She miscarried our child."

Martha looked at him sharply. He didn't realize it, but this line of conversation troubled her more than the couple thinking they were married. They had talked about the two children that had almost been his several times. But until now, seeing him with this baby and observing just how much he actually adored children, she had never realized just what this might mean to their future relationship. Chilling fingers of apprehension surged up her spine.

Had his wife had a medical problem that prevented them from having children, or did he? Fear crashed around Martha like a tidal wave.

He could possibly still father children, could still have a chance to have the babies he loved. Shouldn't he be courting a younger woman—one who could give him children should they marry? It was only yesterday that he thought she was ten years younger than her actual age. Until a few years ago she would have still been able to bear a child.

"I'm sorry," Luke murmured.

Leo nodded. "It was one of our greatest sorrows. We had wanted a whole house full of kids when we married. But when my wife became sick, we understood why she had never been able to—"

He broke off, and Martha felt chilled. It had been because of his wife that he—this man who was so good with babies—hadn't had any of his own. And now he was getting involved with her—another woman who couldn't give them to him, but this time, because of the biological passing of time.

"Well, you may borrow ours whenever you want," Melissa said, relieving the mood. Leo chuckled.

"That's what I do all over the world. It's really not all bad." He scrunched up his nose. "Especially when it's time to hand the baby back to her parents for a change of diapers."

"Oh, no," Melissa groaned, reaching for the little one. "She didn't!"

"Hmm." Leo chuckled. "She did."

"Yep, Mom," the boy confirmed and got up from his seat to place more distance between himself and the smelly baby. "She did."

❧

Not even plaguing thoughts about children were able to mar the return trip to Olympia. Serenity seemed to grow on the vegetation that the car sped past.

The coastal valley slept in the summer way of peace. As Martha gazed out the window, it seemed to her that the other three seasons of the year existed just for this one. The night was a harmonious synchronization of the physical world that was a special treat to their senses. Martha was glad when Leo abandoned the air-conditioning in favor of the night-scented air. Oregano and thyme mixed with that of the pine and eucalyptus trees that sashayed their scent down upon the earth, causing her to draw deep, rejuvenating breaths. And the flowers, hundreds of different ones, created a bouquet that no perfumer in the world could ever hope to recreate.

The town of Ancient Olympia was mostly asleep when the high-powered engine purred its way down the main road. Martha glanced at the clock on the dashboard. It was past one in the morning. It didn't seem any later than ten.

As Leo pulled the car to a stop in front of Once Upon A Time, her comfortable, content feelings found expression in the soft sigh that escaped her lips.

He turned to her, and his eyes crinkled at the corners in the way she liked. "I agree with that."

She laughed softly. "It was the most wonderful birthday I've ever had," she murmured for at least the hundredth time. Reaching up, she placed her hand against his cheek. "Thank you, Leo."

He caught her fingers and planted a soft kiss into her palm. "No, thank you. Since Susan died, holidays of any sort have been difficult for me. Maybe if we had been blessed to have had those two children who were almost ours. . ." He sighed.

Feelings of inadequacy flooded back in, wiping out all the contentment that the ride home had lent to Martha. She had watched him with Melissa and Luke's children. If any man should be a father, it was this one. He shouldn't be wasting his time with her, a woman past childbearing years. He should be dating a younger woman, one who could give him the children he so obviously desired. Wasn't procreation one of the main reasons for marriage, after all?

Even though she was breaking on the inside and her throat felt like dry toast, she had to agree. "Having those two little loves would have made a big difference, Leo." She licked her lips, unsure as to whether she should go on, the topic being deeply personal. But she knew that she had to. Before they took their relationship any further, this was something they had to discuss. "You're a man and. . .you can still. . .have children. If"— her voice dropped to a whisper—"you have the right woman."

His eyes widened, flickered briefly with an intangible hope, and she knew what he was asking.

She lifted one shoulder in a sad shrug. "We met a few years too late for that."

He leaned across the seat, and his husky voice was like a caress. "And yet, I most definitely have the right woman. The only woman. . ."

His warm lips met hers in a touch that was firm and persuasive, not demanding response, rather, giving one of love and reassurance that his feelings for her did not depend in any way on her ability to give him children.

But hope had flickered in his eyes when he'd thought that there might be a possibility that she could still conceive a child.

She had seen it. And the look of disappointment that had flickered briefly before he had deftly smoothed it away, leaving only the grim set of his jaw to indicate that her reply wasn't the one he had wished to hear. It was an impression she would not soon forget.

She squeezed her eyes shut to keep the tears from sliding out. This was not the moment to express sadness over their future—a future she felt almost certain now they couldn't have.

She had somehow known all along that something would keep them apart. She just hadn't thought that it would be something so insurmountable as her age. She had thought it would be her resistance to the change being married might bring to her perfect life. Now she realized just how surmountable that problem was.

With prayer.

In fact, it came as a bit of a shock to her to realize that, having turned over all her to God doubts about the change that being married could bring, she hadn't actually thought about it much in several days.

Could she do the same with this problem?

She knew that she had no alternative. Other than discussing the situation with Leo, that was the only thing to do.

But she wouldn't talk with him about it tonight. They were still on their birthday celebration.

And he had just told her that it was the first holiday that he had enjoyed since he'd lost his wife. She wouldn't let anything mar it. Any discussions about this could wait for another time.

Any time, other than this one.

And. . .only after much prayer.

twelve

During the days following their birthday, Leo doubted that the ancient winners of the pentathlon could have gone around Olympia feeling any better than he. Even though the earth was at one of its most charming stages, it seemed to take on an even more special glow as his love for Martha grew stronger and deeper. They went everywhere together and talked about everything, both serious and frivolous. And although he sensed that there was something on her mind that she wasn't discussing with him, he had been married long enough to Susan to know that when a woman was ready to talk about something, she would.

Susan had always prayed about serious topics before discussing them with him.

He knew that Martha was the same: a similarity between the two women that was as striking as it was admirable. How many problems among couples—in the world in general— could be prevented if everyone prayed to God before voicing them? He would be patient. He would neither pry nor push. And, as had often happened between Susan and him, the problem—or at least most of it—would probably be resolved through her prayer time with God.

They were sitting at a café under a reaching plane tree, enjoying the sweet, natural air-conditioning the ancient deciduous afforded, when he asked something he thought she might enjoy, "How about a bike ride this evening?"

Clink! Her demitasse coffee cup met its saucer too

quickly. He thought it was a testimony to the quality of the porcelain that neither the cup nor saucer broke.

"A. . .bike ride?" she choked out. It was not the response he had expected.

He frowned. "You have ridden before, haven't you?" Cycling was such a large part of his life that he couldn't imagine anyone not doing so.

She laughed, a self-depreciating sound that made him instantly regret his insensitively put question. "I think it might be better to say that a bike, with the help of a mountain, has ridden me." She grimaced and, holding up her hand to keep his question at bay, quickly explained. "The first—and last—time that I was on a bike was when I was about twelve. My older brothers were determined that I should learn. The contraption had always scared me a bit—all that chrome and metal with parts sticking out in all directions seemed daunting."

He chuckled. "I've never seen a bike quite like that." He had always seen it as a streamlined work of engineering.

"Well, my moments on the bike proved that my impression was correct." She paused, and even though her eyes were trained on his, he knew that she wasn't looking at him but rather into the memory of her first and last bike ride.

"Amazingly, after only a few moments I seemed to have perfect balance on the two-wheeled wonder, so much so that my older brother let go of my seat. I found myself pedaling down the main street of our village without the umbilical cord of his grip on the seat. Those first few moments were like a dream."

She sat back, and he could tell that she was reliving the perfect sense of freedom while bike riding. It was one he knew well. "I was going so fast, my waist-length hair flew behind me like a cape, and I felt so"—she shook her head—

"I don't know, free."

"Ahh. . .now that's definitely what riding a bike is all about."

Her face instantly clouded. "But the dream soon turned into a nightmare. I found myself at the end of the village, where the road dipped sharply on its meandering trip to the valley far below. It was then that I realized that I didn't know how to do two very important things." She laughed sourly. "I didn't know how to turn the bike, but even more, I didn't know how to stop the contraption."

"Oh, no."

"Oh, yes," she replied. "I could hear my brothers and all the children of the village running behind me, shouting instructions. But I was too terrified to decipher their words, and the cacophony of their voices just added to the out-of-control feeling of my headlong flight. My front wheel hit a rut in the road, which made the bike turn to the right. The next thing I knew I was no longer on the paved road but flying through a field on the steepest, most direct, and fastest way down the mountain."

"I guess you were about to set a world record for speed," he commented wryly.

She laughed. "It sure felt that way. I probably would have, if the front wheel hadn't then hit a rock, and I learned one way in which to stop a bike. Fast."

He winced. "You didn't."

"I did. But, hey, it wasn't all bad," she laughed. "Other than getting to see how it was to ride a bike, I also got a lesson in flying. I flew about ten feet through the air—but at the time it seemed more like ten miles—before landing on my left shoulder and severely cutting both my knees."

"Ouch."

She kneaded her left shoulder. " 'Ouch' doesn't begin to

describe how my dislocated arm felt. Nor the burning skin on my knees. But the physical pain wasn't anything compared to the damage done to my pride that day. It was a mortifying experience, one in which I have no desire to put myself again."

"But, Martha, haven't you ever heard the saying, 'When you fall off a horse you've got to get right back on and ride again'?"

"If it had been a horse," she countered, with all the logic of a person raised in the country, "I would have gotten back on, dislocated shoulder and all. A horse is a living, breathing creature, and I wouldn't want to hurt its feelings nor have it think it had bettered me."

That wasn't exactly Leo's point. "The idea is that you shouldn't let something like a fall defeat you. Not when you are giving up something as wonderful as riding a bike." He flashed her the most endearing grin he could muster. "Especially, Darling, when riding a bike through the countryside around Olympia with me."

&

"Darling?"

The part of her heart that had been without a love of her own for so many years jumped within her when he called her by that endearment. A fog of swirling, happy feelings inundated her.

"How about if I teach you to ride?" he asked, and *poof* the fog disappeared. His offer had caught her off guard. She hadn't expected it. Hadn't really wanted it, either.

"I don't know, Leo. . ." To have fallen and made a fool of herself when she was a girl of twelve was one thing. To chance doing the same thing now was an entirely different situation.

He leaned back in his chair and eyed her thoughtfully. "Please, Martha. I love cycling, but to have you by my side, as we ride the country lanes together, would be perfect."

"By my side. . .together. . ." They were two phrases that had the same effect on her as the endearment or whenever he told her he loved her. It made her melt inside. To ride a bike with Leo by her side seemed like a very pleasant thing to do. And since cycling was so important to him, shouldn't she at least try to ride again?

"We live in a valley, so you don't have to worry about a mad dash down a mountain," he pointed out.

"That's true."

"I want you to experience the wonder of riding a bike, Martha." He spoke with passion. "It's something so simple, and yet one of life's greatest pleasures. To my way of thinking, anyway. The exhilaration of knowing that the speed you are going is one your legs, along with kinetic energy, make and to feel of the wind in your face—"

"I feel plenty of wind just walking around here during the blustery season," she pointed out.

A throaty chuckle emanated from him.

With patience he said, "You know it's not the same thing." His voice dipped to that low timbre, a cross between a growl and a gentle caress, and she wondered how any woman could ever resist its charm. She knew she couldn't.

"I know," she admitted.

He reached across the table for her hand. "I promise, Darling, that we won't go any faster than you want to."

Looking at him, while feeling his thumb run in a one-way motion across the back of her fingers, she couldn't help but wonder if he were speaking on two levels.

Was he referring to more than just riding a bicycle?

To their relationship perhaps?

Somehow she thought that he was. And the idea filled her with warmth. She so wished that their relationship never had to change from what it was right now. Staying as they were meant that she would never have to face other issues: most importantly, that of not being able to give him a child. She continually gave that conflict over to God, but other than indefinitely remaining a romantic, dating couple, she didn't see any way around it.

She wanted to talk to Leo about the problem again. But until she resolved the issue in her own mind, until she prayed it through thoroughly and felt peace from God about it— something she knew from experience would eventually, one way or the other, be hers—she wouldn't.

"What would my first lesson be?"

A big smile filled the lines around his mouth while a complimentary twinkle flashed in his dark eyes. "How to stop, of course."

Martha didn't attempt to hide her smile. "Of course." She paused. "I really would like to learn, Leo. Not much has ever defeated me, and it goes against my core to be afraid of something, especially something little children do so easily."

"That's the spirit."

"It's always looked fun to me. I've always been particularly fond of pink bikes with white wicker baskets. I think I might look for one like that. Imagine riding to the farmer's market and filling up a basket with flowers. . ."

She could tell from the way a smile played around his mouth that that wasn't quite what he had in mind for their cycling ventures. But he didn't seem to mind. "You're adorable, you know that?"

She guffawed. "A woman my age cannot be described as

adorable, Leo," she challenged. *Especially not with the confused thoughts I have.*

"I disagree," he returned. "What has age got to do with the concept? To be adorable means two things. Either you are worthy of adoration—and that is reserved for Christ alone— or you are delightful and/or charming. That, my dear, brave Martha-Mary, describes you perfectly." He looked at her with that special gleam in his eye. "You are the most delightful and charming lady I know."

As his dark eyes focused on her lips, a faint tremor quivered through her. "You flatter me."

"Ah, Martha-Mary. But don't you know I would much prefer to be kissing you?"

Martha knew because that was what she wanted too. "Would you settle for teaching me to ride a bike?"

"For now," he returned, his voice low and soft, just as she liked it. "For now."

thirteen

Martha knew now that although having the love of a man like Leo might make her world a bit more complex and confusing, it definitely made it nicer too.

And it was because of her love for Leo that she could better empathize with Stella's pain at the loss of Dimitri. Her heart went out to her young friend.

Stella put on a brave face by day, but Martha was often awakened by the soft sound of Stella's sorrow finding expression during the deep hours of the night. It was more a feeling than a sound actually, a motherly intuition, a change in the atmosphere of the house, that told Martha tears fell from her young friend's eyes. Knowing Stella as well as she did, Martha knew that it was better to uphold the girl in prayer rather than offering an embrace, as her arms ached to do.

But after several nights, Martha felt certain that her prayer for the right opportunity to talk to Stella was being answered. Slipping her feet into her sea-foam green slippers, she donned her light summer robe and went to the girl's room. Deep in mourning for her lost love, Stella didn't hear her until she spoke. "Stella, would you please join me on the veranda for a cup of chamomile tea?"

Startled, Stella hastily swiped at the tears that glistened in the moonlight on her cheeks. She reached for her travel clock and, seeing the late hour, offered, "It's the middle of the night, *Kyria* Martha."

"The best time for a heart to heart I'd say."

"But—"

"No buts. I've sensed your pain every night. I've prayed for you until I knew that sleep had given you release from your distress. But tonight the air is sweet, the stars are shining down upon us, the crickets are singing, and God has placed within my heart a few words to share with you. Words that only a woman who has lived for more than half a century without the love of a man has the right to tell a young woman such as you." She paused and softly finished with, "Will you please join me?"

Kicking aside the eyelet sheet, Stella pulled a tissue from the nearly empty box on the night table and sitting up nodded. "To be honest, I think I would like that."

Martha smiled. Of course Stella would. God knew what was in the young woman's heart. "I'll put the kettle on," she said and went toward the kitchen.

When Stella emerged a few minutes later, Martha couldn't help smiling. Dressed in a long T-shirt with a smiling kangaroo, she looked like a young teenager. But Martha knew that her appearance was deceiving. The heart of a woman beat fast and true. And some man one day would be very blessed to have all the love this special young woman had to give, wanted so desperately to give.

Martha had already opened the French doors that led to the vine-laden veranda off the kitchen. Picking up the wooden tray arrayed with her tea service and fresh butter cookies, she motioned Stella outside.

The young woman stood for a moment at the railing, looking out over the sleeping village of Ancient Olympia. Martha watched as she took a deep breath, then another, before turning her ever-observant eyes up toward the heavens.

The big dipper could easily be picked out, but it was the earth's own galaxy, the Milky Way, cutting across the zenith, a long cloud of snowy light, that drew Stella's attention. "Such a big world," she murmured.

"Yes, *kali mou*, it most certainly is," Martha agreed, as she poured the tea into the teacups. She had always liked the soothing sound the liquid made, like a softly flowing brook, as it was transferred from pot to cups, but now, during the deep of the night, even more. "And it's from the God, the Creator of that wonderful sky filled with stars and other worlds, that we who are blessed to be called His children should derive our happiness. Not from any other relationship."

Stella's slender shoulders sagged. "You're talking about Dimitri." Her voice had a deflated sound.

"No, *kali mou*. I'm talking about any relationship. Our worth shouldn't be derived from which town or country we hail or which church we attend, or school, or whose daughter we might be or our bank balance or even"—she paused to let the last have added weight—"which man might love us. Our worth comes from our relationship with the One who created that expansive night sky and"—she held her hand up to her ear to indicate the multitude of insects that were singing all around them—"the littlest creature that crawls upon the earth."

Stella's chin dropped to her chest, and Martha knew she was trying hard not to cry. "My head knows that you're right, *Kyria* Martha," she replied softly. "But my heart—"

She balled up her hands and, holding them against her chest, bent over, as if she had been struck. "My heart just doesn't want to listen to reason. I miss. . .Dimitri. . .so. . .much. If only. . ."

Placing the teapot on the table, Martha wrapped her arms around Stella and gently pulled her up so that she stood straight. She wished she could wave a magic wand and take this hurt away from her. If any woman in the world deserved happiness, it was this slender one. But Martha knew that people often didn't know the difference between what they wanted and what they needed.

"If only. . ."

But Martha wouldn't let her dwell on what would never be, a treacherous route to take. "There are no 'if onlys' in life, Stella. If onlys are as fleeting as the foam upon the sea. If onlys are deciding we need something rather than allowing God to decide if that is how our life is to go. If onlys kill contentment in our life faster than weed killers do the weeds in our gardens. And worse, they kill the knowledge of knowing that we are living in God's will even if an answer to a prayer is not the one we had hoped and wished for, like children wishing upon the first star they see in the night sky."

"But. . .I hurt. . .so badly." she choked out, and Martha could feel the tension take over the muscles in her slender body. "Physically." She placed the heel of her hand against her forehead. "Mentally. . ."

"I know, Dear, I know," Martha massaged her tense back muscles. "But right now is the time when you must let your spirit draw its strength, its courage, its counsel, from God's very own. His Holy Spirit will uphold you through this as He did nine years earlier when your mother passed away. Remember what the Lord said in the Gospel of John about the comforter, the counselor." *Dear Lord, help me remember the words. Please.* She so seldom could recite verses, but she so desperately hoped she could now.

And she did. They just seemed to flow from her mouth. " "And I will ask the Father, and he will give you another

Counselor to be with you forever—the Spirit of truth. The world cannot accept him, because it neither sees him nor knows him. But you—"'"

Stella raised her hands, and Martha panicked that not even those words of the Lord's—the very ones that had most strengthened Stella all those years ago—would help her sorrow this time. But when Stella turned her gaze to the infinite sky, even though tears still glistened on her lashes, like drops of morning dew upon pine, Martha could see the faint flicker of hope. "'"But you know him, for he lives with you and will be in you. I will not leave you as orphans; I will come to you."'"

"I knew you would remember," Martha murmured. "Rather than allowing pain and its debilitating consequences to rule you, let God's courage take ahold of your heart. But most of all, *kali mou*, be courageous and strong and ask yourself if you should accept Dimitri not loving you as coming from God."

"I don't have the courage to ask that," she answered faintly, casting her gaze downward again. "Not yet."

Martha placed the palms of her hands on either side of Stella's small face until the young woman looked up. "Listen to me, Stella." Her throat was tight with welling emotions. She loved this girl—the daughter of her best friend—so very much. "You are the most courageous person I know. Even when facing the death of your mother and infant sister, as well as the despair of your father, you kept your family together. You were indeed your mother's *stella*, her star, who made sure that the children she loved more than life itself were safe. You and your courage did that for your father, your brothers and sister, and for your mother, who relied on her little Stella."

"This is different."

"Yes, it is different," Martha agreed, shocking a response from

Stella in the widening of her eyes. "This is easy compared to what you, a girl of thirteen, did then. This is understanding with a woman's heart that a man, realizing something is missing in the way he is supposed to love you, breaks off your relationship. And it's trusting that God probably has someone else picked out for you, someone who will give you what Dimitri cannot give, is unable to give because"—she ran her hand gently down her cheek, trying to impart comfort—"he is not the man for you."

Tears spilled from Stella's eyes again. "But I'm not like you, *Kyria* Martha. I want to be married. I yearn for it."

Martha stood back. Her concern turned to shock. It reverberated through her. "And who said I don't?"

"But. . .you've never married. And from what you just said about a person's worth coming from God—"

"My worth will come from God whether I remain single all my life or not. I'm not waiting for a man to give me my worth, and neither should a man wait for me to give him his. Marriage has nothing to do with that. Marriage is about companionship; it was designed by God to be the closest and best of all human relationships. God made man and woman to complement one another physically, emotionally, socially, and, most important of all, spiritually."

Stella swiped at her tears and looked at her in the direct way that, in spite of the disquieting turn of their conversation, warmed Martha's heart. This was the Stella she knew, a young woman with bright, inquisitive eyes. Not downcast, anguished ones. "Has that man come into your life? Is it Leo?"

Martha answered carefully. "Our relationship hasn't reached the point yet where we've discussed a future that includes marriage." They had alluded to it but never talked about it. "And even though you and Dimitri dated for years, neither did you reach that point with him. And that's the reason, for your own peace of mind, and to make room in that big heart of yours for the man God does have in His mind for you to marry, that you must let Dimitri go."

Anger jumped into Stella's eyes. "But I don't want to let him go," she grated out, her voice militant. "I won't."

"You must," Martha returned.

Stella's eyes hardened. "Could you, *Kyria* Martha?" she shot back with equal candor. Her eyes were like shiny hard jet, but there was no malice in them. Just pain. "Could you let go of Leo, should you have to?"

Martha took a step back as if she had been slapped. She felt the full force of Stella's ache then. It wasn't just an ache but an agony. The very thought of losing Leo made Martha feel as if something had poked through her skin, her muscles, the bone of her chest, and pierced, with just its tip, her heart. And she knew at that moment that she could never let anything as silly as fearing the changes to her life marriage to Leo might bring come between him and her. There was really only the issue of a child to consider. . . It was quite a revelation. And a freeing one.

Leaving Stella's side, she walked to the railing and let her gaze roam the sleeping world. It was peaceful, perfect, a starry summer night. And she drew strength from it to answer Stella's question, as she knew she must.

"If for some reason Leo had to leave me, or he decided that he didn't love me"—*or because I am barren and he decides that he really desires children*—"I would let him go, Stella. My heart would hurt, but it wouldn't break, for I would continue to live my life as I always have." She turned back to Stella. "I would live it in the knowledge that my relationship with a man does not define who I am." She touched her hand to the beating of her heart. "I'll admit that I've learned these last few weeks that to have a man—to have Leo—in my life is a wonderful thing, a tremendous blessing, something much greater than any of my fanciful daydreaming even thought it to be."

Her confession drew a small smile from Stella's sad face.

"But the greatest blessing is in knowing that I stand approved by God with or without Leo Jones in my life. And it's God who sustains me, not my relationship with any man. Even the one I love."

Stella nodded. "I appreciate your honesty, *Kyria* Martha. It's not fair of me to come into your home and be so unhappy while you should be basking in having the gift of such a love. And after so many years of patience. Patience I know I wouldn't have. And you are right. I must—"

She broke off, squeezing her eyelids shut to stay the tears that were always close by. But she couldn't. They dropped like liquid weights.

Martha went to her and wrapped her in her arms again. Placing her head against her shoulder, Stella whispered the words, which Martha knew, were some of the hardest she had ever said. "I must. . .finally. . .let Dimitri. . .go. And trust God to choose a man for me."

Martha breathed out a silent prayer of thanks. This was a major breakthrough in Stella's recovery, and Martha knew that the strength and determination of her young friend, and her faith, would indeed help her to let go of the man she had loved forever.

Planting a kiss upon the top of her head she whispered, "Yes, *kali mou*, you must."

fourteen

That their late night talk seemed to have done some good was evident in the days that followed.

True to her declaration, Stella made an effort to let Dimitri go, as she seemed to will thoughts of him as far apart from her as he was physically. Although there were still moments when shadows would cross Stella's sweet face, Martha felt sure that her young friend's healing was progressing with a rapidity that only God could have brought to her hurting soul.

When Petros, Stella's father, called a few days later to check up on his daughter, Martha was relieved to be able to tell him that Stella was on the mend. Even though Petros had never considered Dimitri and Stella a good match, he had always feared that his daughter would never let go of the man. Martha was glad to hear the relief in his voice. Even after nine years, Petros was still mourning the loss of his wife, Emily, and there was only so much a man could bear. Guilt that he had wronged his eldest child after Emily's death weighed heavily on his mind.

❧

Casting a glance around the shop, as she always did on first entering each morning, Martha gasped. Her gaze immediately zoomed in on the shiny new bicycle with the big pink bow that sat beside the fireplace in the living area.

"Happy late birthday," Leo said, as Stella stood by his side, clapping her hands and laughing in delight.

"Leo?" She skipped over to the bike and ran her hands over the smoothness of the shiny chrome. "It's beautiful." It was pink and white, the bike of every girl's dream for Christmas morning. "I don't know what to say. It's perfect and—" She giggled when her eyes spied the white wicker basket in front of the handlebars. It was overflowing with a bouquet of flowers. "A basket!" she lowered her face to the flowers and inhaled. "I see you have already gone to the farmer's market!"

"No. Not without you. Those were bought at a florist's."

"Leo, I don't know what to say." She put her hand on the bike's soft seat, which was a little bit higher than her thigh. The seat of the bike she had ridden in the village many years past had come up to her waist at least, maybe even her chest. "It even fits me."

"Of course it fits you," he said, as he came to stand by her side. "It was specially ordered from a shop in Athens just for you. And see"—he pointed to various aspects of the bike—"it has suspension, twenty gears for ease of pedaling, and it's made of titanium, which means it's light but strong. All the things a proper mountain bike needs to traverse the bumpy roads of Greece."

He was so excited that she almost didn't want to say anything to burst the happy bubble he seemed to ride. But she knew that she had to. "Leo, it's wonderful. But when I told you I don't know how to ride, I mean. . .I. . .really. . .don't. . . know how," she said, emphasizing each word. Maybe she hadn't made that totally clear the other day when they'd discussed her previous bike-riding endeavor. Did he know what he was getting in for?

"But didn't we already agree that I would teach you?" His dark eyes focused their attention on her lips, and a faint tremor quivered through her. "I'll teach you everything you need to know," he said, and she wondered, as his warm lips touched upon her own, if he was only talking about teaching her to ride a bike.

But her senses were soon so overwhelmed by the sensation of his nearness, her mind no longer questioned anything—whether she was right for him in spite of her inability to bear children, or anything else. She relished the feeling of being adored by a man. By this man. When the kiss ended, she knew that she had never felt more womanly than she did at this moment. Nothing—not her pretty clothes, not the weekly hairdresser appointments, not even her luxurious baths—gave her that sense of fulfillment from being in his arms. It was a gift for which she thanked God—especially since it was something she had never expected to experience.

"May I?"

Her eyes narrowed. "May you. . .?" What was he asking?

"Teach you to ride this little bike."

Of course. The bike. She nodded. "I'd like that. But I feel so bad. All I gave you for a birthday present is a needlepoint."

"All?" His brows came together, cutting a straight line across his forehead. "Darling Martha, that needlepoint of our spot at the ancient church ruins is so much more than just a bike. It's something you created, a work of your hands." He took them in his own and touched each finger. "Something of you had to go into each stitch to make it so beautiful. I'll cherish it forever. And not only me, but generations long after we are both gone will too."

But to have generations, there must be children.

There are children, Martha. A calm voice of reason returned. *Natalia's little baby will be as your grandchild, and because of Leo and your love, that child will be Leo's grandchild too.*

She took a deep breath. That was what she had to remember, what she had to focus on.

"Your needlepoint is real and good." He kissed the tip of her nose. "And next to your love, it's the most wonderful gift you could have given to me."

Children would have been the most wonderful gift.

But again willing away that nagging thought, she brought her arms up and around Leo and hugged him close. "I love you, Leo."

He rubbed his cheek and jaw against the top of her head, and she felt a slight tremor go through him as he whispered back, "And I love you, Martha."

"Okay, you two," Stella said and laughed, making both Martha and Leo grimace at one another self-consciously. "Enough of that. Go teach *Kyria* Martha to ride a bike, why don't you?"

"I'd like that," Leo said, reaching for Martha's hand. "But I can't." He twisted his wrist and glanced at his watch.

"Already trying to get out of the lessons?" Martha bantered.

"You wish," he said and tweaked her nose. Then, on a serious note, one that sent alarm through Martha's system, he said, "A situation has come up with my company, one that requires a computer conference. It's to start in about half an hour."

His company. Of course. He kept it so separate from their time together that Martha often forgot that he worked at it from his home each day.

"Isn't it the middle of the night at your home office?" Stella asked.

"It's late, but not the middle of the night. But this conference will take place from several locations around the world, so many of the men and women will be going to their computers at odd times."

"But since you're the boss—"

"I got to choose the time," Leo finished and grinned. "So, Martha, your bike lesson will start this evening."

But Martha's mind really wasn't on her lesson. It was on his company. "I hope nothing too serious has come up with your company, Leo." *Nothing that will take you away from me*, was what she wanted to say.

"Don't worry; this conference should be able to handle it." He kissed her lightly. "The wonders of the computer age." And turning away, he tossed over his shoulder as he walked out the door, "I'm quite partial to it."

❧

"Wow!" Brian said as he walked into the shop a few hours later and saw Martha's new bicycle. "What a cute bike! I haven't seen one with a wicker basket in years."

"Why, thank you, Brian. Leo gave it to me. A late birthday present."

Brian rubbed his hand over the shiny new handlebars then sauntered across the room toward the cash register and both Stella and herself.

"Hi, Stella," the young man greeted her.

"Hi." Stella returned and dipped her head slightly. Her shyness around Brian was so acute that Martha was sure had she been as light in coloring as Brian, her cheeks would be bright red.

Seeming to understand and wanting to relieve her, Brian flashed his smile while turning toward the colorful glass beads that one of Martha's Needlepoint Ladies had handcrafted and painted. "Do you suppose that you could help me select some of these, Stella?" he asked and turned back to her.

Stella's eyes widened like Needlepoint's when she was frightened. Always before Brian had settled for her monosyllable replies and hadn't asked anything more of her. Martha was glad that he seemed to want to push her out of her shell now.

"Of course." Stella put aside the ledger she had been writing in and walked to the array of baskets with beads. Martha noticed that she still held on to her pencil. From the grip Stella had on it, Martha was afraid she might unwittingly break it in two. "What do you want to make from them?" she asked, slanting her eyes toward him. When he flashed a bright smile, she lowered her eyes back to the beads.

"I don't know exactly," Brian admitted and let his fingers slide through their smooth coolness as Stella looked on.

Looking at the two, Martha thought they made a lovely, if contrasting, couple. Brian's hair was wavy and nearly red, and he had happy freckles across his face, complimenting his extroverted personality. Stella's hair was dark and straight, her skin smooth without even so much as a mole on her cheek, somehow fitting her serious and introverted personality. But even with their differences, they seemed to fit together like two pieces of a jigsaw puzzle. They complemented one another.

"What would you suggest?" he asked, and Martha's mouth quirked. She was certain that Brian didn't need help in selecting beads. Martha hoped he would succeed in bringing out the woman who had obviously captured his fancy. Stella needed a fun-loving man like Brian in her life, even as just a friend.

"It depends on what you want to make, the colors you want to use, and. . .and. . .the amount of money you want to spend," Stella answered softly. But her answer seemed to give Brian hope. Martha suspected that it was the most she had ever said to him.

He turned and looked at Stella directly. Stella had no

choice but to look up at him. "A necklace," he said after a moment. "One with green and gold"—his playful gaze roamed Stella's face—"that brings out its natural sparkle."

"I. . .see," Stella answered slowly and turned back to the beads. "Well, we have quite a nice selection of green glass beads in right now and these cloisonné," she held up the round beads of enamel work in which the surface decoration had been formed by thin strips of wire. "You could intersperse spangles on the strand, which should make it pick up light and sparkle quite nicely."

"Good idea. I like sparkle in. . .necklaces."

"Okay," Stella reached for a small plastic bag. "How many ounces do you want?" She picked up the little scoop.

"Ten beads."

"Only ten?" Stella turned to him in confusion. "I thought you were going to string a necklace out of them."

"I am."

"You will need more than just ten."

"I'll come and buy more after I string these first ten." He held up his hands and wiggled his fingers around. "I doubt that these thick fingers of mine will be able to do more than that each day, anyway."

Stella's gaze lowered to his hands, and she frowned. "Your fingers aren't thick. They're slender and—" She clamped her mouth on the rest of her sentence, but Martha was almost certain Stella had nearly said nice.

"Okay, ten." She counted out a variety of green glazed beads, gold spangles, cloisonné, a package of thread, and, after sealing it shut, handed the bag to Brian before retreating behind the cash register to ring up the sale.

Nodding at the new bike, Brian asked of Stella, "Do you ride?"

Stella glanced at Martha, who could tell her friend wanted to say no. But that would have been a lie. At medical school, Stella used a bike to go everywhere. Not only did she ride, she was very good at it. Due to traffic, the roads of Athens were not biker friendly. Only the very best dared to brave them.

After a moment she gave a quick nod.

"Would you like to go for a ride sometime?"

"I. . . I don't have my bike here."

Martha looked at her sharply. They both knew that it was arriving by bus later that week. They had discussed only that morning how they could ride together, after lessons.

"A walk, then?" He glanced down. "Your legs are both here."

The chimes rang at the door, and Stella swallowed her reply, looking relieved. She used the distraction as an excuse to ring up the sale at the register.

Martha couldn't help but be pleased as well when she saw that it was Leo. He strode toward her, tall and vigorous, a smile splitting his strong face. She moved from behind the table and walked into his arms. "Hello, Martha-Mary," he said, kissing her lightly.

"Leo." She breathed his name. "Is everything okay with your company?" She had been thinking about his conference all day, concerned that something to do with his business— of all things—might take him away from her for good.

"Everything should be fine."

"'Should be'?" If that was meant to reassure her, it didn't. Apprehension slithered up her spine.

"Really, Darling. I think we managed to get everything sorted out. It's nothing to worry about." Over her head Leo,smiled a greeting at the other two. "Hey, Brian. Stella. How are things going?"

Martha frowned. Had he turned to them as an excuse to drop the subject? He'd said not to worry. . . .

But more than that, God didn't want her to worry. She would give her fears over to Him. And trust both Him and Leo to work out their future. Every aspect of it—her current fear of Leo's work having to take him far from her, her old fear of not being able to give him children. . . She would give everything. . .again. . .continuously. . .through prayer. . . over to God. Or at least she would try very hard to do so.

Brian's infectious laughter returned Martha's attention to the present. He dropped some euros into Stella's hand and held up his beads for Leo to see. "I just wanted something fun to take my mind off scholarly things."

Leo frowned at the little bag. "What's in there?"

"Beads. To make a necklace."

"A necklace for someone special?"

Brian laughed again and tossed the bag a couple of inches in the air as he walked toward the door. "You never know," he threw over his shoulder just as the door closed behind.

Leo beamed. "I really like that guy. He's always so happy."

"He is," Stella whispered, and when both Martha and Leo turned to her, she shrugged shyly. "He seems so uncomplicated, so. . .I don't know, nice."

Leo slanted his eyes toward Martha and smiled. She smiled back. Wisely, neither commented. Martha hoped that Brian wouldn't get tired of trying to draw out the girl. Stella was finally responding.

"Are you ready to start your lessons?" Leo asked, surprising Martha.

Stella smiled. "Go for it, *Kyria* Martha," she encouraged. "I want you to learn so that we can bike ride together."

"It seems to me"—Martha looked toward the door that Brian had just exited—"that someone else wants to do that with you too."

A bashful smile flittered across Stella's face. "Maybe when my bike arrives I will go for a ride with Brian," she admitted, making Martha's heart thrill at how healthy it sounded, in terms of Stella's getting out and getting to know a man other than Dimitri.

A Japanese-speaking couple walked through the door, and Stella looked over at them. "Now go learn to ride. I'll hold down the fort," she said, as she moved toward the pair that were looking at a display of ceramic vases, replicas of those found in the archaeological site just down the road.

Leo walked over to the bike, relieved it of its bow, and pushed it toward the door. "Shall we?"

Martha lightly touched her hand to her stomach to still the butterflies that had taken flight. The idea of riding a bike still terrified her. Even such a friendly looking, Martha-sized bike. "Promise you won't let go of the seat until I'm sure of what I'm doing?"

"Scout's honor."

She breathed out deeply and, waving to Stella, preceded him out the door.

≈

She soon found out that her butterflies were there for a reason.

Even though they found a nice quiet spot to learn and the frame was better proportioned than the one from her childhood; and even though Leo ran beside her patiently, giving her instructions and valiantly holding on to the seat of the swiveling bike; and even though it had a white wicker basket filled with flowers, it was still a bicycle. And it took her days of lessons before she felt confident enough to allow Leo to let go of her seat. And several more days until she could do more than ride in a straight line before stopping the bike, getting off, and turning it around in order to go in a straight line down the dirt path again.

Getting up the nerve to turn the bike to the right or to the left was almost as traumatic as allowing Leo to let go of the seat. And she doubted that she would have ever done that if the front wheel hadn't hit a root on the path and twisted the handlebars in her hands so that she either had to go to the right or fall. So then she could ride in a circle, but only in one direction. It took her several more days until she could turn the bike to the left. And several more days after that until she could go to the right, then to the left, at will. But the big day finally came when Leo decreed that she could officially be called a bike rider and that she could actually go out on the quiet streets.

Martha wasn't so sure about that but didn't want to disappoint him. She hoped that her clothes might give her the confidence she lacked, so she dressed for the big adventure in a fitted, cap-sleeved, cotton, navy T-shirt; khaki cotton twill pedal pushers, and brown leather sandals with turquoise beads. She donned her pink-and-white bike helmet, rather than her normal straw hat, and went to meet him.

"Don't you look. . ." He paused, glancing at her ensemble. "Nice."

"What's wrong?" Martha looked down at her clothes.

"Don't you think you should continue to wear your sneakers?"

She lifted her right foot to show him the rubber soles. "These should be fine." She flashed him a smile. "And don't they look much better than sneakers?"

"I like your sneakers."

"But my feet get so hot. Let me try riding with these. If I don't feel comfortable, I'll change."

"Okay, but let's go back to the field so that you can get the hang of cycling with sandals," he said, nodding at her footwear in a none-too-pleased way.

"All that dust," Martha cried. She had had enough of that field. It might be flat and devoid of traffic, but the *Meltemia*—summer winds similar to the Californian Santa Anas—was late this year, and dust blew everywhere. She had had to soak for nearly an hour in bath-oil beads each evening to feel like a woman again—and not like a prickly porcupine. "No. I'll go slow."

His brows rose in doubt, but he nodded. "Okay. But be careful. People don't realize it, but shoes make a big difference when riding a bike. Your pedaling perception can change with footwear, and it's easy for your foot to slip off the pad."

And that was something she soon found out when, after only thirty feet, her right foot slipped out from under her, got caught in the spokes of the back wheel, and she found herself tumbling to the hard pavement.

"Agh!" Her rump hit the road with a bone-rattling *thump*. She lost her hold on the handlebars and watched, as if in slow motion, as the bike continued on a teetering, weaving, lumbering gait down the road without her.

"Leo!" she cried. Even though she well remembered the last time she had fallen, she hadn't remembered it hurting quite so much as it did now. Her whole body throbbed.

But then, Leo was by her side. "Martha!" His hands reached for her, cradled her. "Don't move until we find out if anything is broken."

She gave a shaky laugh. "Just my pride," she said, as she saw people come running from every direction. "I should have listened to you. . .I should have worn sneakers." She looked down at her pretty sandals. They were askew, with the blue turquoise beads scattered all across the road. But it was her right ankle that got her attention. It seemed to be screaming at her and made her forget the bleeding cuts on her left elbow and shoulder and the scratches that seemed everywhere except, thankfully, her head.

"No, Darling. I shouldn't have given you a present that you could hurt yourself on. I should have insisted that you wear sneakers—" But he stopped speaking as she bent toward her ankle, and his eyes widened in concern. "What is it?"

"My ankle. . .it hurts. . ." Tears sprang to her eyes at the sharp pain that seemed to pulsate from it. She clutched at his shirtsleeve. "It. . .really. . .hurts, Leo." She couldn't help the groan that came out. The muscles in her foot felt like they were tearing apart.

"Let me see." The ridge of his jaw was grim.

"Do. . .you. . .think I. . .broke it?"

"I don't know, but I think I better get you to the hospital to have it X-rayed."

"Oh, no," she groaned.

"Let me through!" Stella's competent voice reached Martha's ears. The most Martha could offer the concerned young woman as Stella knelt by her side was a wobbly smile. After a commiserating return one, Stella was the competent professional. She ran her hands over Martha's body, and Martha knew that she was seeing the side of Stella that would turn her into one of the best of physicians.

"It's her ankle," Leo supplied.

Stella nodded but completed her exam of Martha's more important organs before moving to the ankle. Her touch was light but capable. "Can you move it?" she asked. Even though it hurt to do so, Martha was relieved to see that she could.

"I don't think it's broken. Just badly sprained," Stella pronounced. "But for now—" She spoke to the crowd that had gathered. "The sooner we get ice on it, the better. Can anyone get ice for me?"

"Here." Brian extended his unopened can of icy cola. "Use this until I get an ice pack from the kiosk," he said, then took off for the pack.

Taking it with a grateful nod, Stella applied the cold cola to Martha's ankle right where it was swelling.

"Can she be moved?" Leo asked, concern lacing his voice.

Stella didn't answer him but gave Martha a reassuring smile. "How do you feel, *Kyria* Martha? Do you hurt anywhere else? Your back, your neck, your hip? Anywhere?"

Martha focused on each of those areas as Stella listed them. Except for the jarring pain of her body having been thrown to the ground, she didn't think anything else hurt too badly. "I don't think so."

"Do you want to try walking?"

"No," Leo interjected. "I'll carry her." Looking at Martha, he asked, "If that's okay with you."

Martha nodded. "I would be grateful. Are you sure I'm not too heavy for you, though?"

Leo chuckled. "You're a lightweight." His eyes darkened with of loving concern, the best medicine in the world to Martha. "But even if you weighed as much as a horse," he continued, "I would still be able to carry you."

Brian returned with an ice pack. "The man at the kiosk

also gave me a stretch bandage." He looked over at Martha and grimaced. "He said lots of tourists seem to need them."

She smiled her thanks for trying to lessen the blow to her ego, as Stella expertly tied both the bandage and the ice pack around her ankle.

"If you can just wrap your arms around my neck," Leo instructed after a moment. But that was easy for Martha to do. A natural instinct. She felt herself being lifted from the pavement and, for the first time since she was a little girl, carried by a man. She rested her head against his chest and listened to the rhythm of his heart. It worked as a tranquilizer.

But suddenly remembering her bicycle, she swiveled around. "My bike!" It was on its side in the middle of the road, fresh flowers scattered. The white of the wicker was now black in places. The back wheel looked bent and flat, with several spokes sticking out like spiked hair. "Oh, my bike. . ."

"I'll get your bikes," Brian said, as Leo started walking back toward the shop. All the people—townspeople and tourists alike—offered her a speedy recovery.

"My beautiful bike. . .that you gave me," she whimpered.

"The bike is the least of our concerns right now. It can be fixed." He spoke through clenched teeth. "Not only did I insist that you learn to ride—something you really didn't want to do—but I gave you the instrument of your torture too."

"She'll be fine, Leo," Stella said from their side. "I don't think she even broke her ankle. Just sprained it."

"But it was caused by the present I gave to her."

Martha heard his tone, and even though her leg hurt, she knew that his irrational guilt probably pained him more. "Stop that now, Leo," Martha instructed. "Stop it right this minute," she repeated, when he looked down at her. "If I had worn the correct shoes, we would even now be sailing down the country roads. It's my fault. And as soon as my ankle heals, I will get on the bike again and take not just one but many bike rides with you." She grimaced. "But with the correct shoes this time."

He bridged the two inches that separated them and kissed the tip of her nose. "You are quite a woman, Martha-Mary. You know that?"

Suddenly Martha didn't feel even one of the hundreds of screaming nerve endings in her body. "No. But I don't mind you thinking that."

He laughed and motioned toward all the people that had shown concern for her. "Me and how many others?"

"But you. . .in a different way, I think."

His eyes darkened. "Yes. Me in a very different way."

fifteen

Martha was relieved that the medical station in Ancient Olympia had an X-ray machine—one of the many presents to the community from Leo. She was grateful that she didn't have to go to the hospital, but even more, that her fall in the street hadn't ended with a broken ankle. It was only sprained, as Stella had thought. She was told to stay off it for several days to give the ligaments around her joint time to heal.

"But how am I going to do that?" she complained to Leo a couple of hours later, after all her cuts and bruises had been tended and her ankle wrapped in a fresh bandage. She was on the long couch in Once Upon A Time, with her leg elevated. "I'm not a 'stay off it' kind of woman, and I have the shop to think about," she grumbled.

"Bah," the deep, rasping voice of her father answered from the doorway, and Martha's shocked gaze flew to meet his. "Stella is a competent young lady, and she will look after your store while I will look after keeping you from getting too bored for the next couple of days."

"*Baba*," Martha exclaimed and held out her arms to the slender man as he approached. He leaned down and kissed her on her forehead. As always, his beard tickled her nose. "How did you know? I wasn't expecting you until tomorrow, for my name day."

He winked at Stella, who sent him a conspirator's smile as

she rang up an item on the cash register. "A pixie girl told me about your accident."

Martha smiled at Stella. "I'm glad." She squeezed her father's hand.

He rubbed his other hand against her face. "Did you honestly think that we wouldn't come? Especially since I was as close as Kastro? I returned from New York yesterday."

"What do you mean by 'we'?"

The chimes jingled as Allie, Stavros, and their children, as well as Petros, Stella's father, and her younger brothers and sister came flooding in. "Us!" Jeannie Andreas, the oldest of Allie and Stavros's children, shouted out, speaking for them all. Laughing and chattering, everyone gathered around Martha and Stella. All the children had bouquets of flowers from the hillsides of Kastro for Martha.

"Oh, wow," Stella squealed, as she hugged her father, sister, and brothers. "I can't believe you're all here."

Martha smiled over at the family. She knew how much Stella had been missing them. She had planned to visit them for St. Mary's Day, which was Maria Stella's name day too. But with Martha's sprain, that wouldn't have been possible now.

Martha looked at her father, and tears sprang into her eyes.

He knew her so well. When she had had an appendectomy a few years back, they had learned that the best way for her to forget her pain was to have company all around her. Some people liked quiet. Not Martha. The more people around, the better. But what was she going to do, stuck on the sofa with her foot propped up on pillows?

"Now before you start worrying about looking after us all, we have all checked into the Olympia Hotel, and our needs are all taken care of. The only thing we want is to take your mind off being laid up for the next few days."

"Well, that's not the only thing." Allie spoke from the foot of the sofa. "As your doctor, I want to have a look at that leg," she said, and they all laughed.

Martha's eyes searched out Leo. He had stepped back to let her father and friends gather round her. He was looking at the scene with that of wonder mixed with a poignancy Martha didn't really understand.

"Leo." She extended her arm toward him. When he reached her side, she took his hand and said, "I would like for you to meet my father, as well as some very dear friends." To her father she said, *"Baba,* this is Leo Jones." She winked at him. "You might remember, the man you told me about last May. . ." At his quizzical frown she continued. "You know, the one you said you have been praying about for many years."

Martha had always thought that there wasn't anything that could surprise her father. But she knew then that she had found the one thing.

In the quick way she had inherited from him, her father swiveled around to face Leo. He looked at Leo from above his glasses, a mannerism he used when studying something of much interest or importance. Then he nodded. "Yes, Martha-Mary, I can see that he is," he said, sizing up Leo in the way eighty-five years of living and making people his business had taught him to do. Extending his arm in greeting he offered. *"Heiro poli,* Leo."

Leo returned the salutation meaning "nice to meet you" in perfect Greek. *"Heiro poli, Papouli."*

Baba's eyebrows rose higher at the perfectly spoken greeting before falling again below the rim of his glasses. Martha had told Leo in the past how everyone, with the exception of her brothers and sisters, referred to her father as *Papouli*— grandfatherly priest. She was pleased that he had remembered. "You speak Greek. But you aren't Greek, are you?" *Papouli* asked.

"No, Sir," Leo replied, again in Greek. "I'm American."

"Ha!" *Papouli* exclaimed. "So is Natalia's husband."

"So Martha-Mary told me."

The older man's one eyebrow rose at the use of the double names. "Do you live in America?"

"No, *Baba.* Leo lives here. In Ancient Olympia."

"Ahh." Between his beard and mustache, a smile lit the old man's features. "Of course you do. Your Greek is superb." Turning to Martha he said, "I'm glad for you, *kali mou.* Even though Natalia visits Greece often and has a lovely home in America, I know that it's hard for her to be so far away."

Her father already had her married to Leo! It was time to change the direction of the conversation. Motioning to Brian, who was standing next to Stella, she said, "Brian is American too." Introductions went all around, and when everyone quieted down again, Martha asked her father, "Did you have a nice time in America, *Baba,* while visiting Natalia and Noel?"

"A wonderful time. Natalia and Noel are so adorable together and so looking forward to the birth of their baby."

Martha sent a hesitant glanced up at Leo. Natalia could give Noel a child—several children, even. She couldn't do the same for this man. She looked for something in his face that might show that it troubled him. But there was nothing.

To her father she said, "You must tell me all about it."

"I will," he assured, then looked at her with the concern of a father in his eyes. "But you look very tired now. I think you should get some rest. We'll all come back later tonight after you have had a nap."

"I agree," Allie spoke, her doctor persona fully in place. She was holding Martha's X-rays up to the window to get a better look at what the picture showed. "You were very blessed, Martha. I agree with the doctor in town," she said and flicked her French braid behind her shoulder. "Nothing is broken. It's just a sprain that should heal well, if you give it the proper amount of time to rest." She handed the X-rays to Stavros and lightly touched Martha's ankle to examine how it was bandaged. "It doesn't feel too tight?"

"No, it's fine. It doesn't hurt too much if I don't move it."

"It's very black and blue," Leo commented.

Allie nodded. "That's to be expected."

"Do you want to see it?" Martha asked.

"No, no. That's not necessary." Allie looked at Stella. "Were you able to apply ice to it for the first half an hour or so?"

"Yes." Stella glanced at Brian and smiled, a real smile, Martha noticed. One that wasn't overridden with a bashful tilt of her head. "Brian made sure that I had plenty of ice. And fast."

Allie nodded at him. "Good job. That's probably why there isn't too much swelling." Then she turned to Martha. "Just keep it elevated for the next twenty-four hours and try not to walk on it. We'll bring you a pair of crutches to use this evening."

"But how are you going to get up the stairs to your apartment?" *Baba* asked, concern covering the lines of his face.

Martha knew that the only disadvantage to her refurbished traditional home was its lack of an elevator. She had already decided that she would sleep on the shop's sofa for the next few days. She wasn't sure how well she would rest, but she really didn't know what else to do.

Before she could answer, Leo said, "I'll carry her up and down the stairs for as long as she needs, *Papouli*."

"Leo." She looked at him in surprise, delighted at the prospect. One nice thing that had come from her fall—along with her father's and friend's unexpected arrival had been those few minutes spent in Leo's arms when he carried her back to the shop. He had done so effortlessly. "You don't have to do that," she demurred. "I'll stay down here for the next few days."

"No, Martha. You can't rest here. You need your own bed to recover quickly." He looked at Allie. "Isn't that right, Doctor?"

"Absolutely," Allie returned. But a slight twitch around her mouth and a quick glance at her husband gave away her obvious delight in Leo's concern for Martha.

Martha scanned the faces all around her. She could tell that they were all very interested in learning more about Leo. She would gladly tell them. Soon. "But I'm too heavy for you to be carrying me up and down those stairs." Because the building was so old, the stairs were very steep. There was a big difference between carrying her down a flat road and up those steps.

Leo's smile connected with those of the other men in the group in a male way before he turned to her. "Like I said earlier, you're a lightweight. Believe me. Susan was as tall as the doctor here."

He looked at Allie and smiled, and from her peripheral vision, Martha saw *Baba*'s eyes widen in interest. She knew that she would be called upon to do some explaining about Susan soon. "And Susan weighed much more than you do," he continued. "Even at the end. For the last three months of her life, I carried her all over our house. I want to help as much as I can. After all, I gave you the bike."

"But I wore those silly shoes," she countered. "They were beautiful, though," she sighed.

"Shoes." *Baba* laughed, the deep throaty one of a man pleased about something. "Don't worry about your shoes, *kali mou*. "I have a whole suitcase—a big one—filled with clothes and shoes and accessories for you from Natalia."

"Really?" Martha couldn't help how much that pleased her. She enjoyed clothes, but mostly the ones Natalia picked out for her. It was only a hobby for her, though, because her worth wasn't connected to her pretty clothes. She could be without all her lovely clothes tomorrow, and it really wouldn't make much of a difference to her at all. The Lord's words about seeking first His kingdom and His righteousness were words Martha lived by. Her fashionable wardrobe was just a gift she accepted from the Lord, much like a child who accepts a good gift from her father.

"Now if that doesn't make you feel better, what will?" Stella said, and everyone laughed in understanding. "So it's settled," Stella said, continuing the decisive tone that Martha was glad to hear. Since her breakup with Dimitri, she'd been anything but resolute. Martha couldn't help but wonder if having Brian by her side had something to do with it. Even through her pain, Martha noticed how they had been working in accord since her fall. First concerning the ice and the bikes, and now, over at the cash register as Brian helped her with the many patrons who were now in the store. Her accident wouldn't be too bad if it helped to bring these two closer together, even if only as friends. "Leo will carry you back and forth from your apartment to here so that your foot will heal as quickly as possible."

"Yes. So you can wear all the new shoes Natalia sent to you," *Baba* said, bringing titters from the young girls, who recognized a good bribe when they heard one.

Martha held out her hands in defeat. But it was one she was happy to concede. "Thank you, all." Her eyes touched on everyone before weariness assailed her, nearly closing her heavy lids. "My own bed does sound very good right about now."

Leo squeezed her hand before turning to Allie. "What do you say, Doctor? Shall I start my duty right now?"

"Absolutely."

Stella turned to Brian. "Can you mind the store for a few minutes while *Yatrinna*, that means a 'female doctor' "—she referred to Allie—"and I go and fix Martha's room and get her settled?"

"Sure," Brian was quick to agree. Martha could tell from the way his mouth curved and his light eyes twinkled that he was pleased Stella had asked him too.

"Stavros and I are going to take this group to the sea to swim." *Baba* motioned at the children, who were wandering quietly around the shop looking at all its treasures. "We'll come back with dinner this evening and keep you company on your veranda. How does that sound?"

"Wonderful," Martha murmured. "I'll rest much better knowing you will all be returning. Thanks so much for surprising me a day early for my name day. Somehow, something that could have been so bad"—she motioned to her ankle—"has ended up being quite. . .nice." *Really nice, actually.*

"Remember, *kali mou*, 'with God all things are possible,' " *Baba* said, repeating the same verse he had told her to apply to her life the day she told him about her desire to move to Olympia. "He can even take something as nasty as a spill from your bike and use it to bring about good."

"Amen," Allie agreed, and Martha smiled over at her dear friend. She knew that that was a promise Allie had held tightly to when she had first come to Kastro.

After kisses and well wishes, everyone filed out, leaving only Brian and Leo alone with Martha and a few tourists who were admiring the Byzantine icons one of the Needlepoint Ladies had painted. Allie and Stella had gone upstairs to the apartment to fix up Martha's room.

Leo pulled up a chair and sat next to Martha, while Brian busied himself with retrieving a ladder to dust the highest shelves in the room.

"How are you doing?" Leo asked, as his fingers lightly traced her cheekbone.

She reached up for his hand. "It's funny. I should be sad because of my fall and my ankle." She lifted her elbow and grimaced. The deep scrape on it hurt more than her ankle at the moment. "But the only emotion I have right now is gratitude. I feel so loved. By you, by my father, my friends. . ." She motioned upward. "My God."

"Darling Martha-Mary. You are loved. And your father and friends seem so special."

"You seemed almost. . .sad, though, at one point."

He didn't deny it. "No, not sad. Wistful. My parents are long gone. My wife, for the last six years. I didn't have any brothers or sisters, so there's only me."

"No cousins?"

"Not close ones."

And no children, either, that taunting refrain went through her brain. But she pushed it aside and rubbed her hand against his cheek. "Leo, you have family now. Not only mine, whom I will gladly share with you, but everyone in Olympia who loves you."

Shouldn't that be enough? Were children necessary when one was blessed with so much love? Dear Lord, please help me overcome my doubts about this.

"I thank God for bringing me here."

"Me too, Leo." She rubbed her face against his hand much like her cat might. "Me too."

❧

Allie and Stella settled her into her bed, helping her change into her most comfortable summer sleepwear, a cotton gown of soft pale pink, and rearranged the pillows until her leg felt comfortable. Through the slats in the closed shutters, the curtains danced to the strong beat of the dry wind; the cicadas ground out their deep, hot-weather tune; the happy sounds of tourists wafted up from the street, and to these much-loved summertime melodies, Martha slept like a baby. She slept safe in the knowledge that her *baba* and friends were close by and that the man she loved was in the next room, ready to take care of most all her needs.

And that was a trend that was to continue for the next several days. She was never left alone. Since Stella was needed in the shop and Leo had computer work to do, he brought his laptop and, more often than not, sat in the shade of the vine-covered kitchen veranda, working while Martha slept each afternoon. And when Martha awoke, he traded places with Stella and kept an eye on the shop, while Stella helped Martha with her toiletries and dress.

Her name day celebration was, despite her injuries, one of

the best—and the first that she had not prepared from start to finish on her own. Allie, Stella, and her Needlepoint Ladies had insisted on taking care of everything. The shop was closed for the day since the feast day celebrating the assumption of Jesus' mother, Mary, was a national holiday. Except for the *torta*—torte—and cake, they had the entire party catered by a local *taverna*—restaurant, and Martha sat like a princess among her cushions while all her many friends as well as her relatives in Ancient Olympia came to her home to wish her *Hronia Polla*—Many Years. Souvlaki and gyros; fried zucchini and eggplant; ten different cheeses including the snow-white goat's cheese, feta; five different salads; and bowls of fresh fruit—figs, peaches, plums, melons, and grapes—were offered to all, as well as large servings of *torta* and Allie's famous American-styled chocolate cake.

But what Martha enjoyed most was watching Leo interact with everyone. He and *Baba* had become the best of friends. They spent much time together talking about things ranging from the Olympic Games—both ancient and modern—to the latest computer software Leo's company was developing, to *Baba's* research for his book on the early teachers of the church.

But when Leo wasn't with her father, he was with the children. Stella's youngest brother, Vassili, a young teenager whose voice broke endearingly every now and then, had grown into a computer whiz. He and Leo seemed to talk another language as they discussed the world of computers. But Leo was equally at ease with bouncing Allie and Stavros's youngest child on his shoulders. It was bittersweet, watching him with the children. They seemed to be drawn to Leo as if he were St. Nicholas himself. And seeing him with them only reinforced those prickling fears that Leo deserved the chance to have children of his own. It was the only sadness to touch her during the early days of her convalescence and one that she had to continually give over to the Lord in prayer. She knew that when the time was right, she would talk to Leo about it once again. She only wanted to devote more prayer time to it before she did so.

By the time her family and friends returned to Kastro two days after her name day, Martha's leg was feeling much better, even though Allie insisted that she still stay off it for the next several days. Since her injured tendon seemed to scream whenever she moved it the wrong way or applied pressure, those were doctor's orders that Martha didn't have difficulty following. Especially since she had Leo, Stella, and even Brian to help her with the shop.

Martha sat on the sofa in the shop the next afternoon, her current needlepoint project in her lap—one that she had created of the ancient stadium, a very popular item with the tourists. Leo sat on the other sofa reading a newspaper. Martha sent covert glances above her half glasses toward the cash register, as Brian tried to entice Stella out for a bike ride. Her bicycle had arrived the previous day.

"I can't leave the shop, Brian."

"I'll watch it," Leo interjected, looking above the newspaper at the young couple.

"Are you sure, Leo?" Stella asked, and the hopeful expression in her eyes made Martha's heart rejoice. "The cash register can be kind of tricky."

"I know." He had used it several times. "But I've got it down now." He walked to the register, reached for the cell phone, and handed it to Stella—just as Stella had once done to encourage them to go for a walk together. "To ease your mind—and mine—take this, and if I need anything, I'll call you." He gave an exaggerated wink as he went around the table. "Have a great time."

Stella laughed. Brian beamed.

And Martha didn't think she could love a man more than she did the giving one named Leo Jones.

sixteen

A little over a week later Leo walked into the store one morning. Martha looked up from where she stood. . . without her crutches.

"What's this?" That he was shocked to see her in the shop, alone, and standing without aid was evident in his tone. "How did you get down the stairs?"

"Believe it or not, I walked." She held up her hand to stay his ready protest. "I almost hate to tell you, but Allie came by late last night and declared that my ankle is nearly healed. As long as I keep it bound in a stretch bandage and don't overdo it, it should be fine for normal activities." She laughed. "But she warned me, no bike riding—or attempting to do so—for another month."

He chuckled. "I certainly won't rush that." He frowned. "It's wonderful news, but why did you say that you hate to tell me?"

"Because I'm going to miss not having you around so many hours every day, Leo," she replied without pause. She wanted him to know the truth. She didn't want to go back to just seeing him every now and again and in the evenings. She liked seeing him first thing every morning and then for several hours afterwards.

"Darling Martha." He ran his hand down her cheek and smiled that lazy half smile that made her sing on the inside. "Don't you know that nothing could keep me from coming here every single morning now?" His gaze lifted to the apartment above them. "Actually, I wouldn't mind living there with you."

She knew that her own eyes had to have become as wide as saucers.

"As your husband," he said, and the world seemed to stand still.

"What?"

He laughed, that mighty, soft rumble that she rejoiced in hearing, especially since she knew that she was the one who had brought it out in him. "Don't you know how much I love you and that I want to spend the rest of my life with you?"

Tears gathered in her eyes. Happy tears just like her father's, when glad emotion ran through his system. She tried to blink them away. But Leo wouldn't let her.

Lowering his head to hers, he gently kissed first her right eyelid, then her left. Martha felt as if the world had not only started moving again, but that it was now spinning out of control.

"I love you, and I want to marry you," he said, wrapping his arms around her shoulders to pull her close. With a sound beyond words, he captured her lips with his own. Martha felt the fireworks that she had always heard people talk about.

"I love you too, Leo," she whispered back. She rested her nose against his neck, savoring the manly scent of him. Had he actually said that he wanted the marry her? Even though their relationship had been moving in that direction from the very first, she almost couldn't trust her ears. And she learned at that moment that thinking about changing her life by marrying, and actually being offered the opportunity by a man she loved and who loved her were two entirely different things. Emotions totally supplanted questioning thoughts now, but in a healthy way, a good way— the right way.

" 'A wife of noble character who can find?' " he said softly, with loving emotion, quoting from the final chapter of Proverbs.

He took a half step back so that their gazes could meet. " 'She is worth far more than rubies. . . She sets about her work vigorously; her arms are strong for her tasks. She sees that her trading is profitable, and her lamp does not go out at night,' " he said, indicating her shop with a slight twist of his head. " 'She is clothed in fine linen and purple.' " He ran his hand over her fitted sleeveless shirt, which happened to be purple linen, and chuckled. " 'Her husband' "—he smiled the way a woman hopes a man will smile at her—"the man I want to be to you, Martha," he qualified, " 'is respected at the city gate, where he takes his seat among the elders of the land.' "

"Oh, Leo." The fact that he believed her to have all the makings of a such a wife made her feel deeply blessed. She had never thought that a man would feel that way about her.

"Wait." He touched his finger to her lips. "There's more. 'She is clothed with strength and dignity; she can laugh at the days to come. She speaks with wisdom, and faithful instruction is on her tongue.' As has your wisdom and faithful instruction been toward Stella all summer long."

"Leo, I don't know what to say—"

"Shh," he smiled and continued. " 'Many women do noble things, but you,' dear Martha, 'surpass them all. Charm is deceptive, and beauty is fleeting; but a woman who fears the Lord is to be praised. Give her the reward she has earned, and let her works bring her praise at the city gate.' " And please, please, dear Martha, marry me and make me the happiest man alive."

She gasped. There it was, clear and sure and perfect. The question she had thought never to hear and yet, since meeting Leo, somehow had always known she would be asked. And with it, all the uncertainty she had felt about marriage—the conflicts she had been afraid might come into the perfect life she had made for herself by joining her life to his, his business taking him away from her, and even, the greatest of all, her lack of being able to give him a child—seemed to fade away as the peace of God that transcended all understanding finally, after so many prayers, prevailed within her. She knew then that to marry Leo Jones was most definitely God's will for her life. And that which she wanted more than anything else in the world. Leo was the man her father had been praying would enter her life.

Without allowing even a heartbeat more to pass, she wrapped her arms around his neck and didn't hesitate in answering. "Yes! Yes!" she shouted, and as his strong arms went around her, he lifted and twirled her round and round. She couldn't stop laughing, couldn't ever remember being happier.

"Thank you, Darling. Thank you," he whispered in her ear as he held her close to him. "I promise to make you happy. I promise to be the husband you deserve."

"Oh, Leo," she said, as her feet touched the floor once again. "I only hope you are happy with me. After all, I've never been a wife before. And you have already proven that you make a good husband."

Holding her face between his hands, he looked straight into her eyes. With emotion deepening his voice, he said, "You are an answer to many of my prayers. And one even—"

He swallowed, and she watched his Adam's apple move up and down. "One even that Susan made before she passed on."

She reached up and touched his face. "She wanted you to remarry?"

He nodded. "She knew. . .how much I need the companionship of. . .a special woman in my life. She often admonished me to be open to recognizing that woman when God led me to her. You, dear Martha, are she. I knew it the first afternoon that we talked."

Nodding, remembering that she had felt it even then, she took his hand and led him over to the cream-colored sofa. Sitting, she said, "Tell me about Susan and your life together. Even with our marrying, I don't want you to ever think you have to forget her, or your love, or feel as if you shouldn't talk about her. This might sound strange, but I love her for loving you as much as she did and caring for you when I couldn't."

He shook his head and softly, like a feather touch, cupped his left hand over her right cheek. "No, not strange for you, darling Martha-Mary. Normal for you."

Turning her face to kiss his hand, she then took his hand in her own and prompted again, "Tell me about her and your life together." She had often wanted to ask him but had felt that it was too personal. But with his proposal and her acceptance, everything had changed. Nothing was too private to discuss between them now. Nothing.

"When we married, we weren't Christians. Oh, we were traditional ones, having been raised in the tradition of Christianity and not anything else, but we had never made a conscious choice to follow Jesus Christ and to let the Spirit of God rule in our lives."

"I understand what you mean." She did. Many people called themselves Christians without really understanding what joys and wonders that declaration should bring to their lives. And what a commitment it was on their part too.

"I made a lot of money doing something I loved—designing software—and Susan and I, well, we were very good at spending it. Houses around the world, luxury cars, vacations at the most renowned resorts on earth—"

"Wait. Are you still that wealthy?" She knew that to help others as much as he did, and the community of Olympia in general, that he had to be comfortable, but she had had no idea that he was that well off—not "houses around the world" wealthy. His own home was nice, but not spectacular, certainly with nothing to show off such exceptional wealth. But would she expect anything less from him?

He nodded, but with a funny, little twist to his eyebrows. "Even more now," he admitted. "But, Martha, my greatest wealth is that which belongs to all believers, the richness of knowing Jesus as my savior. That's true wealth. The fact that I also have money means that God has entrusted me with a great responsibility, one that I am to use to help as many people that I can. It's a privilege, but also, a tremendous responsibility," he said, and she knew that the accountability he felt over the use of his monetary assets was great. "One much bigger than the running of my company has ever been. To give away money goes against the nature of man. I should know. For years, it went against my own."

Because of what Natalia and Noel had told her—who were both wealthy too—she understood what he was saying. But unlike Leo, Natalia had given of her money from the first. "Wealth doesn't impress me, Leo," she assured him. "Except maybe in terms of how it's used to help others."

He nodded. "I was sure that it wouldn't. Not with your sister being famous and wealthy."

"Natalia is quite well off, but she's not the reason I'm this way. *Baba* is. And it's the same for Natalia."

He grinned. "Now why doesn't that surprise me?"

She returned his smile. "He might only be a village priest, and yet he's the richest man I know. He doesn't have a portfolio declaring his material worth, rather, a "portfolio" of good works that declares his relationship with Christ. He, like everyone who asks, was saved by God's grace through faith alone, but my father's faith has expressed itself in love and obedience his entire life."

She grinned. "He doesn't have monetary wealth, even though Natalia and Noel are constantly trying to change that. But that has never stopped him from giving all that he has."

" "Silver or gold I do not have, but what I have I give you. In the name of Jesus Christ of Nazareth, walk." ' "

As it always did, that verse from the third chapter of Acts, where Peter healed the crippled beggar, made goose bumps rise on Martha's arms. "Precisely."

"Susan and I learned the hard way that wealth didn't make us happy. There was actually no comfort in it at all."

"My father has often said that it rarely brings comfort. On the contrary, it brings problems unless it's used correctly."

"So we learned. It actually turned me into a monster of sorts, Susan too. I felt as if I could rely upon my wealth, and myself, for everything, that I didn't need anything else. Not even God, really."

He paused, but when he spoke again his voice had the sound of a judge's gavel being struck upon a desk. "Then

Susan became ill." Deep sorrow crossed over the planes of his face. "And we learned the hard way what was important in life. In spite of the years in which we had lived for ourselves—only for ourselves, not for God, and certainly not for His people—we were blessed. God granted us several years of living together as Christians in all the wonderful, miraculous meanings of the word. And we really lived life then, lived life as it is supposed to be lived, with God as the King of our lives.

"Money can be such an insidious thing, Martha. It can make people believe that they are strong. But it's really nothing. Faith, hope, and love, the love that came in the form of the incarnate Christ—that's everything. That is riches beyond comparison."

"You're such a wise man," she murmured, and she was glad that she had asked him about his life with Susan. He was telling her much more than she had expected.

"Only because of the grace of God and only after having lived very foolishly for many years. I wouldn't go back to my thirties or forties for anything."

"Not even to see your wife?"

"I will see her again one day, and then it won't be with pain in her eyes."

She smiled. "And that's what makes you one of the wisest men I know. Almost as wise as my *baba*."

"Now there's a compliment." But then, with deep seriousness, he took her hands in his and said, "Martha, from now on, though, you will be my wife. God has brought you into my life now for that purpose."

She understood what he was saying. And she loved him for it. "The Lord said, 'At the resurrection people will neither marry nor be given in marriage; they will be like the angels in heaven.' "

He nodded. "That's right. It's only here and now that we marry, that we need a helper. In heaven the relationship of marriage is not in existence. Susan is not waiting for me there as her husband, only as her brother in the Lord."

"And that will be a grand reunion."

"It certainly will."

"But, Leo, what about children?" She had to hear from his lips, just one more time, that he really didn't mind that she was too old to give him a child. "Are you sure you don't mind—"

He held up his hand and looked at her as if a piece of a puzzle had just fallen into place. "Is this what's been on your mind all these weeks?"

She knew that her mouth had dropped open. She closed it. "You knew?" How had he known? Having wanted to pray about it, except for that time on their birthday, she was sure that she hadn't said anything about it.

"I sensed that you were wrestling with something. I just had no idea it was this. If I had—" He stopped speaking, then, squeezing her hands for emphasis, said, "If I had, I would have told you, Martha, that this is not something that you need to dwell on. It's not an issue with me."

"But I saw that look that passed over your face on our birthday when you thought that I might still be able to bear a child. You were thrilled with the idea."

He shook his head. "If we were ten or twenty years younger, then I would have loved to have had a child with you, Martha. But that has nothing to do with now."

A week ago, she wouldn't have been able to understand what he was saying. In fact, she would have totally misunderstood him. But she didn't now. The power of prayer. . .how she thanked God for His constant presence in her life. So many problems were being avoided by her having gone to God about this situation first. "God has made that clear to me. But, Leo, I have to ask you this question, just one more time—"

"You can ask me anything, as many times as you want, Martha. Anything. Always. Whenever." He assured her.

She nodded. "Leo, you are a man, and you can still have children if you were with the right wom—"

"As I told you on our birthday, you are the right woman for me, Martha. The only woman."

"But you love children, Leo."

"Of course I love children. What's not to love? But I love Formula One racing cars, zebras, and clipper ships too. That doesn't mean I have to have my own."

"Leo, a child is not like any of those things."

"No, of course not, but the point is the same, Martha. I long ago found peace about this issue. I'll be honest; it was one that plagued both Susan and me for years. That's why we decided to adopt the little girl, our little girl."

"Leo." An amazing thought popped into her head. "Why don't you try to find that girl now?"

The way he looked at her, as if she had just told him he won a billion dollars, made her heart beat even faster.

"Martha, I don't know if you will believe me, but even as I spoke the words 'our little girl,' that was exactly the thought that came into my head too."

"Of course I believe you, Leo." Oh, how she believed him! God and His amazing ways!

He stood up and ran his hand through his hair. She could tell that the idea thrilled him. "Do you really think it's possible?

Do you really think that we might be able to find her?"

We. He immediately put them together in this. That little girl, who was now a young woman, was to be both of theirs to search for, to love. . . It touched her deeply. ""'With God all things are possible,"' Leo," her voice husky with tears of glad emotion. "And if He wants us to find her—and something tells me that's exactly what He wants—then we will."

"We didn't give her up, you know, Susan and I. We just wanted her to have a home with both a father and a mother. Susan only lived for three years longer."

"I know, Leo. That's what makes your searching for her even more special. You and Susan went out looking for her all those years ago because you wanted her in your life. And now you and I are doing the same thing because we want her. At least to let her know that there is a couple in a land far, far away who loves her. If nothing else."

"You really wouldn't mind?"

"Mind?" Martha stood. "Leo, what's to mind?"

He gave a short laugh. "And she's eighteen now. That's good, because I honestly don't think, at this point in my life, that I would like getting up during the middle of the night to care for a hungry baby." He chuckled. "God does have a reason for that biological clock."

"Ah. . .now wait a minute, Leo. Are you forgetting that we might just be doing that soon?"

He frowned. "What do you mean?"

"There's Natalia's baby to think about. Since I'm practically the baby's *yiayia*—grandmother—that means that upon marrying me, you will become its *papou*—grandfather. We will be sharing in midnight feedings upon occasion."

"Ah. . .see dear, sweet, adorable Martha." He smiled, a

slow smile of wonder. "You are giving me a baby, after all."

Feeling like the heroine in her very own love story, she whispered, "I love you, Leo. Thank you for loving me."

"Thank you back, Martha-Mary. Thank you and. . .for giving me a family."

seventeen

When Brian and Stella walked into the shop a few minutes later, the young couple might not have been surprised to see the older couple sitting on the sofa enjoying one another's company, but Leo and Martha were definitely taken aback when Brian leaned over and gave Stella a slow, but sweet, kiss on her lips. Brian acknowledged his audience with a happy smile and a good-natured wave before he turned and disappeared out the door. Martha saw that there was an extra spring to his steps that hadn't been there before. And that was saying something because Brian's walk had always had a bounce to it.

Stella nearly floated over toward them, with the look of a woman in love written across her face. Martha noticed that she was fingering a bright, sparkly necklace that hung from around her slender neck.

Martha's and Leo's eyes met. "I think that romance is in the air," Martha said, and Stella giggled.

"It is," she agreed and two-stepped between the displays of the discus thrower and the Byzantine icons, which made her skirt twirl around her legs like an open umbrella.

"Well, well, well," Leo said.

"Tell, tell, tell," Martha trilled, patting the sofa beside her.

Stella skipped over to her side and threw her arms around Martha's neck. She was so different from that night at the beginning of the summer when Stella had arrived at her door, a sad and heartbroken young woman. There was energy in this hug, the thrill of life radiating through her body. And fun.

"Oh, *Kyria* Martha, you were right," Stella sang. "You told me that if I was to marry some day, that it would be to a man of God's choosing and not my own."

Martha blinked. "Wait a minute." She waved toward the door. "Are you saying that you and Brian—?"

Stella laughed the way she had years ago, before her mother had died and responsibility ruled her. "No, no. Not yet, anyway. But since your accident, Brian and I have become very close. Look," she said, pulling at the beaded necklace. It was green and gold and looked as if it had been fashioned expressly for Stella.

Martha frowned. She recognized the beads. They were the ones they sold. "Wait a minute. Those aren't the beads that Brian—?"

"Yes! Yes! Can you believe it? Brian was buying the beads for me." She patted her hand against her chest. "He wanted to make me a necklace! Have you ever heard of anything so romantic?"

"Well, I'll be," Leo said and chuckled from the other side of Martha. He leaned across Martha to get a better look at the necklace. "Nice job too. I always said I liked that young man."

"You were right." Stella sat back and sighed. "You both were." Her lips turned up at their corners. She sighed a content, dreamy breath. "He's wonderful. So full of life and fun." Sadness shadowed her eyes, and her voice lowered. "Even though he's suffered gravely." She swallowed; then looking down at the hardwood plank floor, she explained. "A week after his eighteenth birthday, his parents and twin brother were killed in a small plane crash."

Martha's hand covered her mouth. "Oh, no."

Leo clicked his tongue against his cheek. "That poor boy."

Stella nodded. "Because he had just legally become an adult, though, he was able to become guardian to his twin sisters, who are a year and a half younger than he." She paused again to swallow down emotion that threatened her with tears. "Because of that he was able to keep his family together." She turned her eyes to Martha. "He didn't even have his father to help him as I did. Except for his sisters, who were devastated, he had only himself and. . .his amazing faith in God. He said that that was what got him through." Her voice lowered. "And still does."

"Other than seeing him in church each Sunday, I thought I saw the stamp of Christianity on him," Leo murmured.

Stella nodded. "He has a fantastic working faith. One that is much stronger than mine."

"Don't say that, *kali mou,*" Martha admonished. "You were only thirteen when your mother died."

Stella shook her head. "No, not that. Lately. With Dimitri, I mean. Thank God Dimitri is an honorable man. I shudder to think what might have happened to me if his scruples weren't so high."

"Call him sometime and tell him that you understand now why he broke up with you. He's been very worried about you."

Her eyes widened. "He's called and asked about me?"

"Of course. He loves you. . .as a friend," Martha was careful to qualify.

Stella nodded. "As I do him. I will call him. Soon." A bright smile lit her face. "I only hope that a fun-loving and joyful woman might soon come into his life. He needs someone like that as much as I needed Brian."

"I hope so too," Martha murmured. Dimitri was still one of Martha's favorite people. "But what's going to happen now that summer is almost over? Is Brian returning to Philadelphia?"

Stella beamed up at her. "No! That's why I'm so happy today. He just told me that he's going to definitely be working at the American School of Classical Studies in Athens this year. That will give us the time to really get to know one another and see if we are meant to be together as we both feel we are."

"I'm so glad, Stella." Martha hugged her young friend close. "Your mother would be so proud of you, as I know your father is already."

"I'm glad too." Leo interjected and, with a conspirator's wink at Martha, said, "Glad to hear that Brian will be in the country this year because I'd really like him to be at our wedding."

Except for her eyes, which swiveled back and forth between Martha and Leo like windshield wipers on a car, Stella's whole body seemed to freeze. But only for a moment.

"*Zito!*" she shouted, the Greek equivalent of *yippee!* and flew up off the sofa and into their arms. "I'm so happy for you! So happy." After hugs and kisses, she ran to the phone. "We have to call everybody! Oh! Natalia! Natalia is going to be so happy! And *Yatrinna*—Allie—and your *baba!*" She put the phone down. "But first I have to tell Brian." She ran toward the door, then ran back to Martha and, throwing her arms around her again, squeezed her so tightly that Martha could hardly breathe. "Oh, *Kyria* Martha, the whole world is going to be happy for you!"

When she left, Leo wrapped his arm around Martha's

shoulder and pulled her close to him. "I don't know about the whole world, but I certainly am happy."

"Umm. . .me too," Martha murmured.

"You don't mind changing your whole life for me? Sharing your world with me?"

She looked up at him sharply. Did he know how that thought had plagued her before? She couldn't be anything but truthful with him. "To be honest, Leo, in the beginning I wasn't so sure about wanting such a change. I wanted you but"—she motioned to her store, which represented the life she had made for herself, with God's help—"I wanted this too."

"And now?"

She smiled. "Now I know that my life here will be enriched by having you in it. But more than that, you are more important to me than any of this. I love it here, but I love you more. All of this could go away, or I could move away from it." That was something she would never have considered before the remarkable events of this day. But she knew now that it was the truth. Suddenly, even this lovely little spot on earth wasn't important to her when compared to her love for Leo. "But I wouldn't want to go anywhere without you, *agapi mou*—my love."

"Thank you, Martha. That means so much to me." He kissed her forehead. Then, chuckling, he asked, "Were there any other conflicts going on in that lovely head of yours that I should know about?"

"Well," she giggled and admitted, "I was afraid. . .for a time. . .of your work taking you away from me."

He laughed. "Believe me, Martha. That will never happen. I would sell my company before letting it."

"Sell it? Leo, no." She was appalled. "I would never ask you to do something like that. Like I said a moment ago, I can even move with you to Olympia, Washington, if you needed to go because of your company." She was flabbergasted to realize that she really could.

"And leave Once Upon A Time. . . ?"

"If it came to a choice between Once Upon A Time and you, Leo, there is nothing to choose from. Once Upon A Time is just a shop. You are the man I love. The man God has, after fifty-seven years, brought into my life to be my companion, my helper, my love."

"Ah. . .Martha. You are worth far more than rubies. . . and diamonds. . .and platinum. . .and gold. . ." He kissed her nose, then sat up straight. "To be truthful, *agapi mou,* my work isn't even a question any more. After much prayer and careful consideration, I have actually decided to sell my company."

"Leo, no!" She swiveled to look at him. "Tell me this isn't because of me?"

"No." He tweaked her nose. "It's for me, for us. I feel it's the direction God wants my life to go. I'm ready for a change. And I love this little town. It's where I want to live and for the first time since I was nineteen, I will be free of the responsibility of running a rather large company. At the moment I just want to stay and help you run Once Upon A Time, where people representing the whole world seem to come to us."

She snuggled down against his shoulder. She believed him. She wouldn't question his decision about his company. She actually felt like it was the correct one too. "Umm. . .and if we don't want the whole world. . . ?"

"We have only to close our door. . ."

"To be alone. . ."

"Together. . ."

She tilted her head up to look at him. "In our land far, far away. . ."

He leaned down, but just before his lips met hers, he whispered, "From the rest of the world. . ."

epilogue

Five Years Later—Kastro

Hugging the mountainside as gracefully as only very old towns can, Kastro, with its sparkling white houses and red-tiled roofs, gleamed like a necklace of rubies and pearls in the light of the setting sun. But it was the people of the village, who walked and laughed among its little streets and alleyways as they made their way to the square, that were the village's greatest charm, its greatest treasure.

That was something that *Papouli*, who sat in the seat of honor at the front table in the square, knew very well. It was his ninetieth birthday, and friends and family had come from near and far in which to help him—the village priest—celebrate both having lived nine decades on God's earth and the publication of his book.

Lanterns and streamers hung from the centuries-old plane tree with long, flower-bedecked tables set up under it for the festivities soon to begin. *Papouli* trained his eyes upward toward the castle. It sat a stalwart friend to him all these years. He remembered playing among its walls when he was just a young boy, courting his dear wife, Tacia, there before they married, and taking his children up there when they were all still too young to climb up alone. A smile formed between his beard and his moustache.

His children.

All six of them were now happily married with children—and some even with grandchildren—of their own.

Even Martha.

His eyes searched out that dear, dear daughter. They crinkled at the corners when he found her right where he had expected her to be: in the hubbub of all the preparations for the feast that was soon to begin.

His Martha-Mary.

His eyes went to the man who stood beside her, helping her, being her loving companion, just as he had been every day of the four years that they had been married. Leo was the perfect answer to his prayer for a mate for Martha. And then some.

Papouli's eyes went to his newest granddaughter, Helen, who was near her new mother and father, Martha and Leo. He could tell from Helen's animated movements that she was reveling in all the love, not only from her new parents, but also that which the extended family wanted to share with her.

It had taken several years, but Leo and Martha had finally managed to track down the little girl Leo and his first wife had almost adopted so many years earlier. And *Papouli* knew that that had been a part of God's plan too. Helen, twenty-three years old now, had once again found herself all alone in the world when the couple who had adopted her—parents Helen had loved very much—had gone to heaven within months of each other.

Leo and Martha had arrived in her life within weeks of that sorrow, and now she was their daughter, both emotionally, and as of a few days previously, legally.

Papouli's gaze slid over to his Natalia.

He knew from Natalia how wonderful adopting a child could be.

Natalia was playing not only with her own little golden-haired daughter, but with all the children who came anywhere near her reaching, welcoming arms. And there was Stella and her husband, Brian, playing right along with them. Brian had one of his and Stella's twin sons on his shoulders while Stavros held the other. Dimitri and his wife swung their youngest child—a little boy of Indian background—in the air between them. He squealed out in the delighted way of babies secure in their world.

Ahh. . .the happy sounds, Papouli thought as he lifted his gaze up toward the cross that sat atop the dome of the Byzantine church that had been his place of worship for all of his ninety years. The sounds of his friends and family laughing and talking and playing were glorious.

He closed his eyes.

It was like a symphony.

The symphony of life.

Or else it was like one of *Yatrinna's*—the doctor's—much loved fairy tales: Happily-ever-afters sent straight from God had come to all his children and friends.

And with tears of joy glistening in his fine old eyes, *Papouli* said the most simple but most heartfelt prayer of all. "Thank You, Lord. Thank You."

A Letter To Our Readers

Dear Reader:

In order that we might better contribute to your reading enjoyment, we would appreciate your taking a few minutes to respond to the following questions. We welcome your comments and read each form and letter we receive. When completed, please return to the following:

Fiction Editor
Heartsong Presents
PO Box 719
Uhrichsville, Ohio 44683

1. Did you enjoy reading *In A Land Far, Far Away* by Melanie Panagiotopoulos?
   ❏ Very much! I would like to see more books by this author!
   ❏ Moderately. I would have enjoyed it more if

   _____

   _____

   _____

2. Are you a member of **Heartsong Presents**? ❏ Yes ❏ No
   If no, where did you purchase this book? _____

   _____

3. How would you rate, on a scale from 1 (poor) to 5 (superior), the cover design? _____

4. On a scale from 1 (poor) to 10 (superior), please rate the following elements.

_____	Heroine	_____	Plot
_____	Hero	_____	Inspirational theme
_____	Setting	_____	Secondary characters

5. These characters were special because?_____

_____

_____

6. How has this book inspired your life?_____

_____

_____

7. What settings would you like to see covered in future
   Heartsong Presents books? _____

_____

_____

8. What are some inspirational themes you would like to see
   treated in future books? _____

_____

_____

9. Would you be interested in reading other **Heartsong
   Presents** titles? ❑ Yes ❑ No

10. Please check your age range:
    ❑ Under 18   ❑ 18-24
    ❑ 25-34   ❑ 35-45
    ❑ 46-55   ❑ Over 55

Name_____

Occupation_____

Address_____

City_____ State_____ Zip_____

WISCONSIN

4 stories in 1

Can God truly touch tattered lives and heal hearts too heavy to hope? In the state of Wisconsin, four women encounter situations that seem unbearable—challenging their faith in God, in love, and in themselves. Can a broken marriage be renewed? Can God serve as the Husband for an unmarried woman, and as Father of her illegitimate child? Can two wounded spirits rebuild a faltering business—and their ruined lives? Can a lost love really be found again? Join popular author Andrea Boeshaar on a journey of discovery, as four women find a haven of hope.

Contemporary, paperback, 480 pages, 5 ³/₁₆"x 8"

❥ ❥ ❥ ❥ ❥ ❥ ❥ ❥ ❥ 🖤 ❥ ❥ ❥ ❥ ❥ ❥ ❥ ❥ ❥

❥ ❥ ❥ ❥ ❥ ❥ ❥ ❥ ❥ 🖤 ❥ ❥ ❥ ❥ ❥ ❥ ❥ ❥ ❥

Presents

ℋEARTSONG 🖤 PRESENTS

Love Stories
Are Rated G!

That's for godly, gratifying, and of course, great! If you love a thrilling love story but don't appreciate the sordidness of some popular paperback romances, **Heartsong Presents** is for you. In fact, **Heartsong Presents** is the premiere inspirational romance book club featuring love stories where Christian faith is the primary ingredient in a marriage relationship.

Sign up today to receive your first set of four, never-before-published Christian romances. Send no money now; you will receive a bill with the first shipment. You may cancel at any time without obligation, and if you aren't completely satisfied with any selection, you may return the books for an immediate refund!

Imagine. . .four new romances every four weeks—two historical, two contemporary—with men and women like you who long to meet the one God has chosen as the love of their lives. . .all for the low price of $10.99 postpaid.

To join, simply complete the coupon below and mail to the address provided. **Heartsong Presents** romances are rated G for another reason: They'll arrive Godspeed!

YES! Sign me up for Heartsong!

NEW MEMBERSHIPS WILL BE SHIPPED IMMEDIATELY!
Send no money now. We'll bill you only $10.99 post-paid with your first shipment of four books. Or for faster action, call toll free 1-800-847-8270.

NAME _____

ADDRESS _____

CITY_____STATE_____ ZIP_____

MAIL TO: HEARTSONG PRESENTS, P.O. Box 721, Uhrichsville, Ohio 44683
or visit www.heartsongpresents.com